CRY OF
COURAGE

BETWEEN TWO FLAGS

1. *Cry of Courage*
2. *Where Bugles Call*

AN AMERICAN ADVENTURE

1. *The Overland Escape*
2. *The Desperate Search*
3. *Danger on Thunder Mountain*
4. *The Secret of the Howling Cave*
5. *The Flaming Trap*
6. *Terror in the Sky*
7. *Mystery of the Phantom Gold*
8. *The Gold Train Bandits*
9. *High Country Ambush*

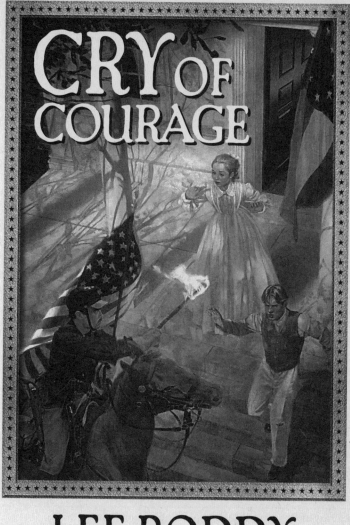

CRY OF COURAGE

LEE RODDY

BETHANY HOUSE PUBLISHERS
MINNEAPOLIS, MINNESOTA 55438

Published by Bethany House Publishers
A Ministry of Bethany Fellowship International
11300 Hampshire Avenue South
Minneapolis, Minnesota 55438

Printed in the United States of America by
Bethany Press International, Minneapolis, Minnesota 55438

Library of Congress Cataloging-in-Publication Data

CIP data applied for

ISBN 0–7642–2025–X   CIP

To Cicely
with all my love
in our very special
anniversary year

LEE RODDY is the award-winning and bestselling author of many books, television programs, and motion pictures, including *Grizzly Adams*, *Jesus*, and THE D.J. DILLION ADVENTURE SERIES, BHP's AN AMERICAN ADVENTURE, and THE LADD FAMILY SERIES with Focus on the Family. He and his wife make their home in California.

CONTENTS

PROLOGUE

From Gideon Tugwell's journal, October 11, 1933

My children and grandchildren have urged me to share with others what it was like growing up in the 1861–65 period of American history, which people today usually call the Civil War.

I still keep the daily journal I began early in that conflict. However, faded words set down nearly seventy years ago now seem as dry and brittle as the pages on which they were written.

So on this, my eighty-fifth birthday, I have taken those memories and tried to breathe life into them by telling the story exactly as it happened to me and to those I knew back then.

To make the story more real, I have re-created those events as if they were told through another person with my name. However, I am the boy Gideon in the narrative, and the others in the story are also ones I knew.

It is my fondest hope that you may see and feel what it was like to have lived with me and other young people in what became America's most bitter and bloody war.

It was a story written in family blood because brother fought brother, father fought son, and white and black races

★ ★

struggled with their relationships. The result changed the course of our nation forever.

So let us begin with that terrible day in April 1861, when I was about the age you are now. . . .

THE SLAVE AUCTION

Gideon Tugwell abruptly broke off his happy whistling and looked back from the high seat on the rickety farm wagon. His gaze swept the empty four-wheeled town coach with the black body, distinctive gold stripe, and Briarstone Plantation crest. A pair of matched bay horses stood in the carriage's red shafts.

Gideon slapped the reins across the brown mule's back in an instinctive reflex to hurry him along. As he twisted to look behind, Gideon's blue eyes darted along the cluster of saddle horses, rigs, and small groups of well-dressed plantation families who stood talking. But there was no sign of William Lodge, the cause of Gideon's concern.

He continued warily driving the family's old farm wagon down the dusty streets of Church Creek, Virginia. He twisted in the high seat to look back again.

A voice ahead called, "Hey! Watch where you're going!" Gideon automatically pulled back hard on the reins and swiveled his head forward just as a boy of about fifteen jumped out of the way.

"Sorry!" Gideon muttered, looking down into the dirty face of Edwin Toombs.

"It's getting so a body can't walk across the street these days," Edwin complained. He was three years older than Gideon and the oldest of several poor white children of the overseer at Silas Lodge's plantation called Briarstone. Gideon, who also belonged to the class known disparagingly as "poor white trash," knew Edwin from irregularly attending the plantation school.

"I didn't see you," Gideon added truthfully.

"Reckon not." Edwin grinned in forgiveness and lifted his slouch hat. He ran a grimy sleeve across his forehead. "But it's a good thing it was me instead of William Lodge, or you'd be eating dirt by now."

"I just passed his carriage, so I was figuring to stay out of his way."

"Well, I see that him and his pa ain't run you Tugwells out of the country yet." Edwin's grin widened, showing crooked teeth.

"They're not going to, either," Gideon replied grimly. He turned in the seat to look back. "What're all those people doing in town today?"

"Ain't you heard?" Edwin stepped a bare foot up on the wheel and into the wagon to sit beside Gideon, who was also shoeless. "Slave auction. Old man Whitman died sudden-like, and his heirs at Glenbury Hill are having to raise cash money by selling his slaves."

Gideon nodded, knowing that such sales were rarely held in April. Most took place in the autumn harvest.

"My pa tells me that William's father is going to buy him a body servant for his fifteenth birthday," Edwin added. "You want to watch the bidding?"

Gideon sighed. "Can't. My pa broke our plowshare, so I'm here to see if the blacksmith can repair it. Pa's mighty anxious for me to get back. Can't do much on a small farm when I've driven the only mule to town."

"Ah," Edwin scoffed, "you're just scared that William will give you another beating."

"I'm sure not anxious to get close to him," Gideon admitted. He secretly wished he wasn't so skinny but more solidly built like William. Someday Gideon hoped to grow big and strong enough to repay William for the blows he had rained on him for years.

"If he's interested in buying a body servant," Edwin commented, "he won't even notice you. Let's at least see part of the sale. It won't take long."

Gideon hesitated, torn between the choices. He wasn't anxious to get home. He hated farming, and he had never seen a slave auction even though he was born and reared in the South. He removed his wide-brimmed hat and thoughtfully ran tanned fingers through his straw-colored hair.

His dirt-poor father never owned slaves, but Gideon had seen them all his life working the nearby wealthy tobacco plantations. Having slaves around seemed as normal to him as plowing a field or hunting rabbits.

Quickly, his eyes skimmed the people moving toward the showroom, but there was still no sign of William. "Maybe if we can go around in back," Gideon decided, "I guess it wouldn't hurt to watch a little bit."

The boys rode around a corner out of sight, tied the mule to a post, and walked back toward an imposing fifteen-foot-high brick wall.

"What does your pa think about Abe Lincoln?" Edwin asked. "Is he bluffing about saving the Union, or is it going to mean war with us?"

"Pa says he expects it'll end up in shooting."

"That so? If it does, maybe I'll be a drummer boy and go off with the soldiers. How about you?"

"Can't. Pa needs me on the farm."

"Too bad. My pa says if it comes to war, our boys will whup them bluecoats so fast that only those of us who enlist right away will get a chance to kill a Yankee. He says the Confederacy won't be forced to stay in the Union at the point of a Yankee gun."

Gideon was a little uneasy as they approached the back of

the wall. They slipped through an open iron gate and stopped to look around.

The thick, high wall, built to prevent slaves from escaping, enclosed a large, empty lot paved with bricks. There was nothing in it but a dreary-looking slave jail, a small, wooden office, and a showroom where the trader's merchandise would soon be displayed to prospective white buyers.

"This place sort of closes in on you," Edwin said in a low voice. "Makes you glad you're white, huh?"

Gideon merely nodded while slipping quietly behind the office building. The jail door opened, and seven barefoot slaves stepped into the yard, the shackles on their hands and feet clanking dismally in the clear April air.

Edwin peered around a corner of the office and nudged Gideon with an elbow. "You ever see slaves dressed up so smart as these?"

Gideon shook his head, studying the pathetic human stock about to be sold. A woman in her late twenties wore a one-piece rough garment tied loosely at the neck. The whites of her frightened eyes were in sharp contrast to her black skin and hair. Three children clung to her.

The youngest, a boy about five, wore an inexpensive suit, as did a boy of about ten, the same age as Gideon's brother Benjamin. Both slave boys trembled in silent fear of possibly being separated from their mother.

A girl about seven wore a bright one-piece garment that she kept touching as though she had never seen such a pretty thing in her life. She held her head high, seemingly unafraid. She whispered orders to her brothers in the way big sisters tend to do. Still, Gideon noticed that her lower lip trembled before she clamped her mouth tightly and straightened the dress.

"I bet they never had on such good clothes in all their lives," Edwin whispered. "I also bet they don't get to keep them, but they come back to the slave trader when they're sold. You wait and see."

★ ★

"They look better than any slaves I've ever seen," Gideon admitted. He remembered to keep an eye out for William, periodically skimming the prospective white buyers casually chatting as they made their way into the showroom. Gideon's gaze returned to the slaves.

There was only one man. He was slightly stooped with age, having almost blue skin and a cap of curly hair as white as sheep's fleece.

"That's Hector," Edwin explained. "My pa told me he was old man Whitman's carriage driver long before I was born. I don't think he'll bring much today. Now, you take that young buck mulatto about my age just coming out the door; he's right prime for a slave boy."

"He's not part of that woman's family?"

"Naw. My pa, being overseer at the Lodge's place, hears a lot. He said that mulatto boy was sold away from his mother and the rest of his family before old man Whitman bought him a year or so back. His name's Nat. Say, I bet that's who William's daddy plans to buy him for his birthday."

Gideon studied the light-skinned slave boy, who stood very still and looked straight ahead with dry eyes. He seemed to neither hear nor feel any of the anguish going on with the mother and her children.

Edwin said, "He's got a strange look for a slave. You notice that?"

"That's because he's not staring at the ground or off in the distance like the others. He's as proud looking as a yearling colt."

The white trader finished his inspection of scrubbed bodies and clean fingernails. He motioned for the woman and her children to go to the right side of the showroom. The old man and the teenage boy moved to the left.

"Now, then," the trader said, stepping back and swinging a gold-headed cane for emphasis, "remember what I said. Don't cry out, no matter what happens, or I'll take the whip to you.

★ ★

"You," he pointed the cane at the woman, "make your pickaninnies let go of you. Have them stop whimpering and stand quiet. Answer polite if you're asked something, but otherwise, keep your mouth shut except for smiling. Look cheerful. Nobody wants a surly-looking servant."

"I couldn't smile if I was going to be sold off like a pig or a cow," Gideon mused. "'Specially the little ones. They may never see each other or their ma again."

"I sure wouldn't like it, neither," Edwin agreed.

The trader started to reach for a bell, signaling his assistant to let the buyers enter the showroom, but stopped in front of the young mulatto. Unlike the others, who stood with eyes downcast, he boldly met the trader's hard gray ones.

"You one of them uppity blacks?" he demanded, menacingly whacking the gold-headed cane across his open palm. He waited, but when the slave didn't reply or lower his eyes, the trader swore mightily. "You need to be taught your place! If it wouldn't bring the price down, I'd lay the leather on you right now!"

As Gideon watched, the slave boy steadily returned the trader's challenging stare. Even when he drew back his open hand as though to deliver a sharp blow, the boy did not flinch or show any sign of submission.

"Uh-oh!" Gideon whispered. "I'd sure hate to be the new owner of that one."

Edwin nodded. "If William buys him, I think he's buying trouble. That would serve him right."

The trader snapped at the youthful slave. "Boy, I got no time to teach you a lesson right now." He turned to his assistant. "Get the doors open and let the buyers check the merchandise."

Gideon and Edwin stayed out of sight, bending low and running along the outside of the showroom to where a partly open, dusty window offered an opportunity to look within.

Gideon glanced around anxiously, trying to keep an eye out

★ ★

for William or his father, planter Silas Lodge. He glimpsed them pushing through the small crowd to stand in the front row before the two rows of slaves. Gideon recognized most of the prospective buyers as well-to-do tobacco planters and some of their wives and daughters.

Gideon and Edwin watched buyers move along the two rows of slaves. He could catch a few words now and then as a planter asked questions of the young mother.

"Can you cook?" When she replied politely in the affirmative, he asked, "Are you a good seamstress?"

Other buyers' voices drowned out her answers as a small group gathered around the teenage slave boy, ignoring the white-haired old man. "You a good yard man?" one white man asked. When the boy merely nodded instead of responding with the usual, "Yes, Massa," another asked, "Can you saddle a horse or drive a carriage?"

Again there was only a brief nod before Silas Lodge's voice rose strong and clear. "You ever been a body servant?"

Gideon couldn't hear the answer or tell if the slave nodded because William and other prospective buyers encircled the boy. They forced his mouth open to look at his teeth. At the same time, William felt the slave's arms and legs.

"Seems firm and sound, Father," William commented.

Edwin nudged Gideon and jerked his chin toward two pre-teen girls in hoopskirts just pushing their way into the front row, where a few women were watching but not buying.

"I recognize Julie, William's sister," Gideon said in a low tone, briefly glancing at the dark-haired girl. "But who's the other one with the long blond curls?"

"Ain't you heard? She's a cousin to William and Julie, recently come from Illinois to live with the Lodge family. Last year Emily's sisters and brothers were carried off by diphtheria or scarlet fever or something like that.

"Then a couple of months ago her parents also died. Her daddy was a brother to Silas Lodge, and so Emily has come to stay with her only living relatives. Purtiest gal in these parts, ain't she?"

Gideon didn't reply as he watched William and his father cross the room to examine the woman. The other buyers followed, momentarily leaving the boy and the gray-haired slave alone.

Anger flushing his face, the trader hurried toward the teenage boy. "What's the matter with you?" the trader demanded in a low tone that carried only a few feet. "You know how to say, 'Yes, Master,' instead of nodding. If you cost me a sale today, I'm going to whip the hide off of you and then throw salt water on the cuts until you learn respect for your superiors. You hear me?"

Gideon admired the young slave's bravery, for he again met the trader's gray eyes without blinking or looking away.

"That's it!" the trader hissed. "I'm withdrawing you from sale. In a little while, you'll wish you were dead!"

"Wait!" The blond girl's voice made the trader whirl around, his eyes glittering with fury.

She shook off Julie's restraining hand and took a few quick steps to face the trader. "Please don't punish this boy for such a little thing."

"This isn't your concern, miss," the trader said quietly. His voice was hard but so low that none of the prospective buyers even looked around from where they were checking out the woman and her children.

The girl's Yankee accent was clear when she spoke again with conviction. "I wouldn't let an animal be treated the way you threatened to treat him," she said defiantly.

The trader took a deep breath as though about to explode, then he seemed to sense some danger. A crafty look seeped into his eyes. He said with sudden politeness, "You talk like a Yankee. Who are you, miss?"

"My name is Emily Lodge. That's my uncle and my cousin over there." She pointed to where they stood with their backs toward her, still talking to the slave mother. "If you touch this boy, Uncle Silas will have you run out of town on a rail!"

"Oh, forgive me!" The trader's harsh tone was replaced with an oily gush. "I didn't realize that."

"Uncle Silas has come to buy a body servant for William's fifteenth birthday," Emily explained. "I believe he's interested in this young man."

At the window, Gideon and Edwin exchanged amused glances while the trader apologized excessively. He assured Emily that he was only joking; the slave boy wouldn't be hurt.

Seemingly satisfied, Emily started to turn back to Julie.

Her face clearly showed shock and surprise at her cousin's audacity. Julie whispered something to Emily, which got the girls into a discussion the boys couldn't quite make out. Julie seemed upset, and as she walked away, Emily glanced around, still distressed over the incident with the trader. Her gaze touched the two white boys' faces at the window. They looked as startled as Julie had. Hesitantly, she walked toward them.

"Uh-oh!" Edwin whispered. "Why's she coming here?"

"I don't know," Gideon replied, glancing toward William, "but I don't like it. If William sees me . . ."

He didn't finish as the girl stepped close to the window. He admired her spirit but couldn't say that.

"Did you hear what that awful man said?" she asked with a toss of her long golden curls. "He's a beast!"

Neither boy replied as Emily continued in a rush of angry words. "I didn't want to come to this awful place, but I'm staying with my relatives, who insisted I attend this with them." She pointed toward the crowd. "That's my uncle and aunt with their son, my cousin. That girl walking away is also my cousin. Now I'm glad I came because that poor boy was saved from a whipping."

When neither boy replied, Emily looked closely at Edwin. "Where have I seen you before?"

"At Briarstone. My pa is overseer for your uncle."

★ ★

"Oh yes, I remember seeing you around. Your name is Edwin, isn't it? Edwin Toombs?" As he nodded, Emily turned soft violet eyes on Gideon. "And you are. . . ?"

"Gideon Tugwell." He almost choked on his own name when he saw William glance up, then do a double take.

"Uh-oh!" Edwin whispered. "Better run, Gideon! Here he comes!"

TERRIBLE NEWS

William outweighed him by about forty pounds. But Gideon had a stubborn streak that sometimes flared unexpectedly. This was one of those times, so he stood still while Edwin spun away and ran across the brick-paved yard.

Gideon waited until William reached both big hands through the partly open window and grabbed for the farm boy's homespun shirt. He took a step back out of reach.

William thrust his angry red face into the window opening. "Come here!"

Gideon swallowed hard before saying quietly, "No. I'm not one of your slaves."

"You're worse!" William groped through the window but could not quite reach the other boy. "You're nothing but poor white trash, and that's all you'll ever be! Now, come here and get the beating you deserve!"

"I've been beat up before," Gideon admitted calmly, "but while you're getting in some licks, I'll give some of my own. Besides, I'm not as afraid of getting hurt as I am of being a coward." His voice seemed to come from far away, as though he were listening to someone else.

Emily reached out a restraining hand and gently laid it on her cousin's well-muscled arm. "Please, William, don't—"

He whirled on her. "I won't have the likes of him speaking to you!"

"I spoke first," she protested. "It's not his fault!"

William glared at her. "I suppose you Yankee girls don't know any better, but you're in the South now. You stay away from him!" He turned toward Gideon. "And you stay away from her!"

Gideon's stubborn streak replied for him. "I don't need you to tell me who I can speak to and who I can't!"

William made another frantic grab for Gideon's shirt just as Silas Lodge called.

"William, the auction's starting. You'd better get over here."

William gave one final angry look through the window. "Remember what I said!" He spun on his heel and hurried toward the auction block.

Emily stood uncertainly, looking at Gideon when he again approached the window. "I'm sorry about this; really, I am."

"Me too. But you shouldn't say anything to him 'cause it just makes him madder."

"I had to," she replied matter-of-factly.

"Thanks." Gideon nodded and watched her turn and walk back toward Julie. From the way she acted, Gideon was sure Julie was scolding her.

Edwin appeared beside Gideon. "That was a bullheaded thing you did. Why didn't you just run?"

"Couldn't. I'd get over a pounding, but I couldn't live with myself if I lit out."

"You sure do have a cussed streak, Gideon. I suppose that means you're going to stay and watch the auction?"

Gideon glanced toward William and his father, who stood in the first row of buyers before the auction block. Behind them, Emily and Julie waited with those who were merely spectators. He caught Julie stealing a look his way. "Yes," Gideon told Edwin, "I believe I will."

Julie placed her hand over her mouth and whispered, "I

think that boy is looking at you."

"Which one?" Emily kept her voice low so her uncle and William couldn't overhear.

"You know, Gideon Tugwell."

"What do you know about him?"

"Really, Emily! You can see for yourself he's an uneducated dirt farmer. Even our servants look down on the likes of such poor whites."

"He's got a firmness of mind and spirit; I'll say that for him."

"Shh! Don't ever let my father or brother hear you say anything like that! They've been trying to buy the Tugwells' property for years, but they're so stubborn they won't sell. That drives Father and William crazy."

The slaver interrupted, stepping up on a raised platform and banging his gold-headed cane on the floor for attention. "You are all in luck today, ladies and gentlemen, because I have for sale the finest stock of servants anywhere in Virginia."

As a hush settled over the crowd, the slaver continued. "As you know, our late good neighbor and friend, Thaddeus Whitman, died recently, leaving in his estate some of the most well-mannered and obedient servants anyone could ask for. His heirs have been forced to sell those servants you see before you. We'll start the bidding on this outstanding young woman aged about twenty-nine."

As the young black mother mounted the stairs to stand on the block, she trembled but kept her head high. The stifled whimpers of her frightened children at the foot of the stairs could clearly be heard by everyone.

The seller continued extolling her virtues as a cook, seamstress, and house maid. He called attention to the many good years of service she could provide her new owners.

"Why isn't he mentioning her children?" Emily whispered.

"Shh!" Julie hissed. "Listen."

The slaver's voice rose to a chant almost like the way

★ ★

tobacco auctioneers' did when Briarstone's crop was harvested and ready for sale. "We'll start the bidding at one hundred dollars. Who'll give a hundred dollars for this fine house servant?"

"One hundred," a man called from the crowd.

"Two hundred!" a bidder next to him said.

"Who'll make it three—?" the slaver began but was interrupted by the woman.

She reached out toward the two white men, urging them. "Please, Massas! Buy my chillun!"

Emily saw the slaver give the woman a warning look, but tears sprang to her ebony cheeks, and her voice rose in an agonized plea. "Oh please, Massas! Buy my chillun, too!"

The first bidder grumbled loudly enough so that everyone could hear, "I don't need any useless little pickaninnies. Four hundred!"

Emily involuntarily gasped and clutched at her uncle's arm. "Uncle Silas, buy her and the children so they can stay together!"

He turned to look sternly down at her. "We only need a body servant for William."

Tears suddenly stung Emily's eyes. She whirled about and blindly pushed her way through the spectators as the bidding continued. She headed out the door into the fresh air, but not before she heard the auctioneer exclaim, "Sold for five hundred dollars!"

As she was led away, his words were drowned out by the shrieks of the woman's children, who knew they would never again see their mother.

At the window, Gideon watched Emily's hasty retreat while Julie ran after her.

Edwin, unmoved, kept his eyes on the mother and the efforts of her desperate children to follow her. "I bet the slaver is going to sell the young'uns off one by one," Edwin commented.

★ ★

Gideon's mouth suddenly went dry, and he felt a scalding mist searing his eyeballs. Quickly, he ran a rough sleeve across his face and eyes.

"What's the matter?" Edwin asked suspiciously. "You got something in your eye?"

"Something like that." Gideon's voice dropped to barely a hoarse whisper.

"It's the natural order of things, like watching calves, colts, or a litter of pigs sold from their mothers," Edwin assured him. "So don't let it bother you."

Gideon didn't answer but blinked rapidly to clear his vision and glanced toward where the girl cousins were standing in the shade of the high brick wall.

Emily had covered her face with both hands and leaned her forehead against the rough bricks. Julie stood helplessly at her side, one arm draped comfortingly over her cousin's shoulder.

"Emily had better not let her uncle or William see that," Edwin said softly. "My pa says Silas Lodge doesn't like Yankee ideas about slaves."

Gideon didn't reply but looked inside the showroom just as the auctioneer sold the slave mother's ten-year-old son. New screams of grief erupted from his siblings.

Still with her face against the outside wall, Emily moaned through tear-dampened fingers, "I had no idea it was so horrible! So . . . so inhuman! How can people do that to other human beings?"

"It's not quite the same thing," Julie replied.

Emily's head snapped up. She wiped at the tears staining her cheeks. "Julie! How can you say that?"

"Well, my father says that it's meant to be. Those black savages are taken from their pagan jungle homes where they know nothing but idolatry. They're brought here where they're taught the catechism and learn how to worship the one true God."

★ ★

Emily's mouth dropped open. "You actually believe that the way those people are treated here is going to bring them to the Lord?"

Her voice began to rise in indignation. "How is that poor slave woman going to be drawn to the God of her master when she is forcibly torn from her children and her family is scattered forever? Where does she, or other slaves with absolutely no freedom, see the love of God presented in a way that makes them want to leave pagan backgrounds to become Christians?"

Squirming, Julie lowered her eyes from her cousin's intense face. "You need to talk to my father about that. He explains it much better than I."

Emily stared. "You grew up believing that, didn't you? But did it ever occur to you to question if that's logical, let alone truthful?"

Julie looked through the open door toward the auction. "Oh, look! They're putting that mulatto boy up that William wants to buy."

"I don't want to watch. In fact, I've seen enough already. I'm sorry I let Uncle Silas and William talk me into coming here in the first place!" Emily turned away.

"You'll get used to it," Julie said, stepping to the open door and peering into the showroom. "They're making him take off his shirt."

"His shirt? Whatever for?"

"To examine his back, of course. If it's nice and smooth, that means he probably doesn't steal or run away, isn't hard to control or lazy. Things like that."

She didn't look, but Emily was definitely curious. "And if it's not smooth?"

"It'll be one mass of scars from where he's been whipped. Nobody wants a slave who's been whipped a lot because it means he's a troublemaker."

"I read *Uncle Tom's Cabin*," Emily replied. "I've also heard

★ ★

lecturers up North say that sometimes a cruel master beats slaves for no reason."

"Shh!" Julie laid a forefinger across her lips. "Don't ever mention that book at Briarstone! And you shouldn't have listened to those lying abolitionists. They're the ones who are stirring up all this trouble."

Emily's tears had been replaced with anger. "How do you know they're liars?" she challenged. "And how do you know whether Harriet Beecher Stowe's book isn't true? Have you read it?"

"Of course not! I shudder to think what Father or William would do if they thought I even knew about that awful book."

Emily's voice softened as she put her arm around her cousin. "Oh, Julie! You and I were such good friends when we were little and before my family moved north. Even after not seeing you these past few years, I felt the same closeness when your family took me in and gave me a place to live. But you and I are so different now.

"You're like most of the Southern women and girls I've met lately," Emily continued. "You're soft-spoken and well-mannered, especially around your heavy-handed father and brother. I was reared to be respectful to my parents, but I was also allowed to have opinions of my own and to express them."

Julie smiled. "I remember even when you were little, before your family moved north, how you would antagonize my father and William by speaking out of turn."

"I don't think it's speaking out of turn. God gave me a brain and a tongue, and I expect He wants me to use them. I can't change; I won't."

"Maybe you'd better." Julie's voice took on an ominous edge. "We're the only family you have left in the world. I'd sure hate to see you turned out for something you said."

Emily stared. "You think your father would do that?"

"I hope not, but why take the chance of angering him? He's got an iron will, not just with the servants but with mother and me, too. You must not cross him." After a pause she added, "Think about what I said."

Frowning, Emily turned to look inside the showroom floor just as the auctioneer brought his hammer down with finality.

"Sold—this fine, strong, and docile mulatto boy for seven hundred and fifty dollars to young Master William of Briarstone Plantation!"

At the window, Gideon and Edwin turned and hurried across the brick-paved yard toward the gate where they had entered.

Gideon shook his head. "Did you hear how the slaver described that boy?"

"Sure did." Edwin lowered his voice to imitate the auctioneer. " 'He's a trained yard boy who can garden, drive a carriage like a man, and spent the last year as a body servant to his late master. This boy is the most docile, obedient black person you'll ever meet.' "

Gideon laughed at the impersonation as he slid through the open gate and began walking down the middle of the dusty street. "There's something in his eyes that says he's no ordinary slave."

Edwin fell into step beside Gideon. "Maybe that's because he obviously had him a white daddy."

"No matter. The law says that the child follows the condition of the mother, and she was black. So he's a slave and always will be. Now, these planters may look down on you and me, but at least we're free. And someday I'm going to be somebody. You'll see."

"Oh? What'll you be?"

"I'm not telling just yet," Gideon replied evasively. His tone hardened. "But I'm not going to be called 'poor white trash' all my life."

"Look out!" Edwin shouted, grabbing Gideon's arm and diving for the side of the street.

★ ★

A rider on a bay horse heavily lathered with foaming perspiration galloped wildly around a corner near where Gideon had parked the mule and wagon. He shouted to the boys as he dashed on toward the men and women pouring out of the showroom floor and into the street.

"Fort Sumter has been fired on!"

"What?" Gideon yelled back in shock, but the rider did not answer or look back.

Disbelief sounded in Edwin's voice. "Did he just say that—?"

"Yes," Gideon interrupted, watching the rider slide his mount to a halt and stand in the stirrups to repeatedly cry out the news to the people standing there. Abruptly, Gideon sprinted toward his wagon. "I've got to get home! The war has started!"

★ ★

DREAMS OF
FREEDOM

Gideon's heart hammered in his chest as he forced the reluctant mule to a slow trot. He could hardly control his excitement as he hurried to tell his father the news about the war.

The old farm wagon creaked and swayed as Gideon quickly left the village and took the turnpike. Soon he turned onto a dusty rural road, passed open countryside and the swamp, and entered the woods before swinging into the Tugwells' hardscrabble farmyard.

The two coonhounds dashed out from under the high front porch and bounded down the lane to meet Gideon.

His father looked up from where he was repairing a leather harness under a small shed. He had removed his slouch hat so his uncombed hair with streaks of gray showed. "What's the matter with you, Gideon?" he yelled angrily. "Are you trying to kill that animal?"

"It's war, Papa!" Gideon shouted, eyes bright with excitement. He pulled back on the reins, bringing the mule, its sides heaving, to a stop. "They fired on Fort Sumter in Charleston Harbor, South Carolina!"

"That's no reason to run that mule so hard!" The man's long chin whiskers bobbed below high cheekbones and sunken cheeks.

Gideon's thrill in being the first to bring the news to his father dissolved into the old tensions. The constant parental disapproval shriveled the boy's soul, but he tried again. "But the Yankees might come here!"

"Well, they ain't here now, and we got planting to finish." His father straightened the suspenders over his shoulders while striding rapidly in his faded, patched pants toward the side of the wagon. "What took you so long to get that plow-share?"

Gideon squirmed on the high seat when his father saw the broken plow part. "This ain't fixed!" he roared and turned furious brown eyes on his son. "Why not? What you been doin' all this time?"

Gideon retreated into the familiar shell of silence and the frustration of never being able to please his father. He certainly couldn't admit that he had watched a slave auction and totally forgot his town mission when he heard about Confederates firing on the Union Fort.

He was saved from more irate reproof when his younger brother ran barefoot out of the small shack with the lean-to in back.

"Gideon!" ten-year-old Ben called, dashing up in baggy pants. "What did you see in the village?"

"Tell you later." He stepped down from the wagon, petted the hounds, and ran a calloused hand over Ben's straw-colored hair, so much like Gideon's.

Their father snapped, "Gideon, run down to the field and tell Isham to come here. You take over his planting so he can go into the village to get this thing fixed. We've already lost too much time."

Gideon nodded and tied the mule to a fence rail. He asked over his shoulder, "You think the army will make him go fight in the war, Papa?"

Gideon Tugwell Sr. glowered at his namesake.

"War?" Ben cried. "What war?"

Gideon didn't feel like explaining anymore; he just wanted to get away from his father.

★ ★

The back door swung open, and sisters Kate and Lilly ran out. "Gideon!" six-year-old Kate cried hopefully. She brushed back an old strip of red cloth that served as a ribbon for her hair. "Did you bring me something?"

"And how about me?" Lilly asked.

Ben spoke first. "He said a war's started."

"What's a war?" Lilly asked as Gideon bent to put his arms around the four-year-old.

Before Gideon could reply, Ben explained, "A war is where men kill lots of people. Isham's old enough he might have to go fight."

Kate gasped. "How come?"

"'Cause he's eighteen," Ben said knowingly.

Little Lilly broke free of Gideon's arms. "Would he get killed dead?"

"He might," Ben quickly told her.

"Ben!" their father warned sternly. "That's enough!"

Kate whirled to dash across the yard, with Lilly shrieking after her. "Mama!" Kate cried. "There's a war, and Isham could get killed dead!"

The father glowered at Ben. "Now you've done it! I ought to box your ears good!" He sighed, then added, "We'd all better go in and talk to your mother before the girls scare her to death."

★   ★   ★   ★   ★

The Lodge town carriage, with its gleaming black sides and distinctive gold stripes, pitched gently as it left the village and headed toward Briarstone Plantation with the mistress, Emily, and Julie riding inside.

Nat, William's newly purchased body servant, rode outside on the seat beside "Uncle" George, the gray-haired coachman. He sat proudly erect, expertly guiding the matched bay team with the sun glistening on their black manes and tails.

Neither man nor boy spoke until the dusty road curved into

★ ★

a line of trees displaying their fresh new leaves.

Uncle George cleared his throat and spoke softly. "Young master told me to show you around when we get to the plantation, so maybe I should start now by telling you something about Briarstone."

Nat turned surprised eyes on the aging coachman. "You speak proper English!"

"Shh! Keep your voice down." George smiled, evidently as pleased with the compliment as he was proud of the bright green livery with the gold buttons on his swallow-tailed coat and matching pants.

Nat had not felt like conversation after being sold on the auction block and knowing he faced an uncertain future as a body servant to a teenage white boy. But his curiosity was aroused at George's words.

"But," Nat replied, keeping his tone low, "I heard you using slave dialect when talking to them a while ago." He jerked his head to indicate the passengers inside the coach.

Smiling, George explained, "That's one of the things I learned in nearly sixty years at Briarstone. The master and mistress expect me to sound like all the other servants—that's what white folks down here call us slaves—so I do that in front of them. But I learned to speak like a white man by listening and then practicing when I was alone."

Nat's dark eyes narrowed suspiciously. "You doing that so you can run away to freedom in the North?"

Chuckling, George shook his head. "I'm too old for that. But sometimes I see a bright young buck with a look about him that tells me he's thinking about freedom."

Nat tensed. "You know somebody like that?"

"Not recently." George took his gaze from the road ahead to look thoughtfully at Nat before adding, "But today I think I met another one."

Nat had determined to never tell anyone about his secret dream. Alarm spread through him like a hot drink on a cold morning. "What's that mean?" he asked bluntly.

"Oh, nothing. I don't think white folks see such things, and most of the servants don't, either. I guess that's because they have given up thinking about freedom. But I've lived long enough to see what some folks don't."

Confusion gripped Nat and he fell silent. Was George one of the spies that the master or mistress on every plantation recruited to spy on the other servants? Was George fishing for information? Or had he really seen something that gave Nat's plans away?

When the silence stretched on, George said, "I've seen runaways chased down by dogs and torn up something awful. That's even before the slave catcher or the master nearly whipped the poor runaway to death. It's a mighty dangerous thing to do—run away, I mean."

"Why're you telling me?" It seemed like a safe question to Nat.

"No special reason. But if you ever meet up with someone who's thinking about it, you tell them to never trust anybody; not even another slave. And you tell that possible runaway that nothing he says or does should give his thoughts away. Sometimes these show up plain as the nose on your face."

"Well, I'm not likely to meet such a person."

"'Course not, Nat." George smiled. "I'm just an old man talking to help pass the miles."

Nat wasn't sure he believed that; not at all. But he leaned back and fell into a thoughtful hush.

Dust swirling up from the road sifted through the carriage windows, settling a fine powder on Emily, Julie, and her mother. Uncle Silas and William had stayed in the village to talk about the war with other plantation owners.

Emily's aunt used a dainty linen handkerchief to dab at the dust on her pale cheeks. Glancing out the window, she heaved a sigh of relief. "We're almost there," she told the cousins. "I

★ ★

can hardly wait to get out of these clothes and wash my hands and face."

"What do you think we should do about the war?" Julie asked.

"Your father will make those decisions."

Emily had ridden in silence, still greatly distressed about the slave mother being sold away from her children. They had all been purchased by separate buyers. Their anguished cries and tears as they were separated, probably forever, still haunted Emily. She could not get the sights and sounds out of her mind.

Julie turned to Emily. "You lived in the North. What do you think the Yankees will do if they invade here?"

Emily tried to ignore the grainy feeling between her teeth. "I don't know anything about soldiers, but I know that Union men are decent, God-fearing people."

Aunt Anna sighed softly. "War changes people."

Emily was surprised at the comment. She asked, "What do you mean?"

"My father was in a war."

"Grandpa was in the Blackhawk War with your Abraham Lincoln," Julie explained. "On Grandpa's last visit here, when all the talk about possible war began, he said he was sure the Yankees would invade Virginia. Then he said we should move away. He meant Mama and me, but now we would take you with us because the soldiers will eventually come here."

Emily turned to her aunt. "Will we do that?"

"Your uncle will be home tonight; ask him."

Emily felt tension building inside at the evasion. Her own mother had always had an opinion, which her husband had respected, although he always had the final say about family matters. Emily's parents had listened to her ideas, too, even when she was little. Looking back, Emily knew that was more politeness than anything else, but it had helped her to think things through and form her own conclusions.

★ ★

In the short time Emily had stayed with her only living relatives, she had become very aware of how different life was at Briarstone.

Aunt Anna never made a decision about anything except the house servants. Uncle Silas was not only master of the slaves but also master of all Briarstone. His wife and daughter were locked into their expected pliant roles in the Southern culture.

Emily leaned back in the seat, wondering how her late father could have been so different from his older brother. Her father, Hiram, had been born and reared in Virginia, yet he had gone north and eventually became what his brother Silas considered a traitor—an abolitionist.

The brothers had never spoken or corresponded after Uncle Silas wrote a spiteful letter to Hiram.

Emily had been surprised that Uncle Silas took her in after death claimed her entire family. Aunt Anna had assured Emily that it was a Christian duty to care for her niece.

That didn't make Emily feel really welcome, but Julie had made up for that. The girls had resumed their close friendship, which had started before Emily and her family had moved to Illinois six years earlier.

"We're home!" Julie announced as the coach turned into the long lane with magnificent old trees that led up to the front door. "I can hardly wait for Papa to get home so we can find out what's going to happen."

Emily nodded, but her thoughts jumped back to the auction. The slave mother and her children were no longer together. But what about Gideon? He must have a family, even though they were obviously very poor. Would they stay or go if Federal troops came?

★ ★ ★ ★ ★

Gideon sat on the homemade bench with his older brother. Ben had run to bring Isham from the river bottom, where he had been sowing seed by hand. Kate and Lilly sat on the floor,

★ ★

occasionally gripping each other's hands at the solemn words of their father and mother.

Ben tapped his fingers on the plain wooden table. "I could be a drummer boy and be right in the middle of battles—"

"Hush, Ben!" His mother gently took his hands in hers. They were still white with flour. She had been preparing to make biscuits when the girls screeched into the tiny kitchen with their war news.

Isham stroked his upper lip, where he was trying to grow a mustache as a sign of his coming manhood. "It will be a short war," he declared confidently. "In the village, everybody I talked to says it won't last more than a few weeks. If we want to kill a Yankee, we got to enlist right away."

His father played with the ends of his beard, which came down to the second button of his faded shirt. "You're talking foolishness, Isham."

"Foolishness?" Isham bristled, his voice rising. "I'm eighteen and old enough to do what I want!"

"As long as you put your feet under my table," his father thundered, "you'll do as I say!"

Martha Tugwell threw up both hands. "Please, stop it! Both of you! We've got to talk this over quietly and sensibly."

Gideon wanted to comfort his mother, but all he could do was stand up and step over to her side. "It's all right, Mama," he assured her. "Everyone's just all worked up over what will happen if soldiers come here."

Isham nodded and lowered his voice. "They'll come here if they're not stopped before then. I'd rather go fight them now than wait until they're here, stealing everything we've got. You see that, don't you, Papa?"

All eyes turned expectantly to the father. At fifty-one, he was twenty years older than his wife, who was stepmother to Isham. "Old" Gideon, as he was known locally, had lost his first wife and two children to disease. He had remarried and reared a second family.

★ ★

"I hate to say it, Isham," he replied, "because I need you on the farm. But you're probably right. You do what you have to. Gideon and Ben will have to double up on the chores when you're gone."

Gideon jerked as if he had been hit. A terrible anger seized him. He had learned to control it for fear of another hard slap. "But, Papa! I—"

Again, his father broke in. "That's all I want to hear out of you, Gideon! You spend all your time chasing butterflies and trying to write stories instead of helping with the chores around here. Now, sit down and let's decide what has to be done to keep them thieving Yankee dogs from stealing us blind."

Gideon's mother whispered, "Better do as he says."

Gideon sank weakly onto the bench again, hearing his father's voice as though it were suddenly far away. He was saying that if the Federals did invade Virginia, they probably wouldn't bother the Tugwell family. Their little house was well hidden in the trees near the river and partly protected by Black Water Swamp.

"However," Old Gideon added thoughtfully, "an invading army will certainly seize everything of value at the plantations, especially Briarstone."

Gideon's mind snapped back. That new girl with the hair like spring sunshine now lived at Briarstone.

Gideon's father continued. "Maybe this will get Silas Lodge off my back. He'll be too busy to keep trying to buy me out or run me off because the invaders can't miss seeing that fancy three-story house. Yankees will carry off food, livestock, poultry, and any valuables in the house. Then they'll probably burn it, along with all the other plantation homes around here."

After pausing for breath, Old Gideon added, "They'll likely burn everything—slave quarters, smokehouse, barns, and other buildings. I just hope Silas has sense enough to send his wife and those two girls away."

Gideon surprised himself by whispering, "So do I."

★ ★

His father glanced sharply at him. "What?"

"Nothing." Gideon took a slow, deep breath and forced away all thoughts about Briarstone. A roaring fire erupted inside his head.

Someday, he told himself fiercely, *I'm going to become a writer. I'll move to New York or someplace big, and I'm never coming back to this place!*

★ ★

PREPARING FOR INVASION

The Tugwell family discussion lasted longer than Gideon expected. Farm work never stopped, but it had to wait till the day after Fort Sumter was fired on. Afterward, Gideon's father sat in his old chair by the fireplace and stroked his beard in silence.

His wife stood beside him. She had washed the flour off her hands, and now they rested lightly on his stooped shoulders. She was only thirteen years older than her stepson, Isham, but Gideon could see the lines already gouging long furrows into her tired face.

Old Gideon gave his beard a final stroke and stood up. "I've decided," he declared with finality. "I never let Silas Lodge run me off this place, and I'm not going to let any Yankee do it, either. Isham, show Gideon and Ben how to do your chores before you enlist."

Gideon silently groaned at the idea of having even more hated farm work dumped on him. But he knew from experience that there was no use trying to get his father to change his mind after it was made up.

Martha asked, "Can the girls and I stay here?"

Her husband glanced at her but didn't answer as his gaze moved on to Kate and Lilly.

Gideon waited, fearful of what might happen if they stayed and the soldiers came. Yet he was almost as fearful of how difficult it would be for Ben and him to live with only their stern father in the tiny house.

"Can we, Papa?" Kate eagerly prompted.

He seemed not to hear as he turned to look out the window at the neatly prepared flower beds.

Gideon's eyes followed his father's gaze. The flower beds would soon blossom with the bright spring colors of crocuses, lilies of the valley, and lilacs. Even the rosebushes were showing signs of developing buds.

All of that was in sharp contrast to the drab yard with its assortment of farm equipment. Martha Tugwell had managed to squeeze time out of her washing, ironing, cooking, and baking to give some beauty to the outside of the family's unpainted wooden shack.

At last, Old Gideon turned away from the window and again faced his family. "Martha, it would be better," he said somberly, looking up at her, "if you and the girls could go visit relatives out of Virginia.

"But we don't know which of those are going to remain in the Union and which will join the Confederacy. I suspect Virginia *will* join, but there's no sense sending you all away when the war might follow you."

Both girls and Ben greeted the decision with happy shouts. They didn't want to be separated from the only home and family they had ever known.

Isham nodded approvingly to his father, saying, "I'll help pick out places to hide things if the Yankees come, then I'll go into the village and enlist."

Gideon felt his father's eyes lock onto him with a silent question. He avoided meeting the gaze while he mentally sank deep into an unhappy black hole. Everyone else seemed satisfied, but he felt himself sliding helplessly into a mire from which there was no escape.

"Well?" his father asked sharply.

Gideon shrugged and nodded. "Whatever is best," he said

★ ★

as noncommittally as possible. But he had also made a private decision: He would leave the farm as soon as he could and go to a city like Richmond. There he could pursue his dream of becoming a writer. But first he had to get more education, and that meant having to again face William at the plantation school on Monday.

★ ★ ★ ★ ★

Uncle George showed Nat around the plantation as he had been instructed. They left the stately three-story "big house" where it stood, solid and square, at the end of a long line of ancient shady poplars. The kitchen was to the right but separated from the manor house both to prevent fire and to keep cooking odors away.

"Where's the covered walkway so the dishes can be carried to the table when it's snowing or raining?" Nat asked.

The old slave chuckled. "There's a tunnel running between the two buildings called the 'whistling place.' Everybody carrying food or even empty plates has to whistle in there to show they're not sneaking a bite."

Nat thought Uncle George was fooling, but a quick glance at his face convinced the boy that was the truth.

"This plantation, like most others, is self-sufficient," the gray-haired guide continued. "Those three houses beyond the kitchen are for sewing, weaving, and spinning.

"To the left of the big house, there's the springhouse with the well, ice house, and smokehouse. Come on, let's walk past the big house and through the English box hedge so you can see everything else."

Nat fell into step with his guide, who pointed out the shoemaker's shop, the dye house, and blacksmith shop.

Nat had already seen the barn, where the carriages and horses were kept, along with chickens, ducks, turkeys, cows, and sheep. A flock of gray geese challenged the intruders with raucous calls.

★ ★

"Geese make great watchdogs," George explained, turning back under the great oak trees with their new leaves showing.

"They're noisy all right," Nat agreed. He pointed beyond the other buildings to a row of shacks lined up to face a dirt road. "Those the slave quarters?"

"Yes, but you won't have to live there. You'll stay in the big house, where your young master can have you fetch and carry for him, like a dog."

The words rankled Nat. He scowled and shot back, "I'm no dog!"

"I didn't mean to offend you." George sadly shook his head. "Some folks working the fields from dawn to night think they'd like to live near the master and the mistress. But house slaves are watched every minute. They have to sleep outside their owner's door or curled up on the stairs or someplace else real close. So will you. I'm glad to sleep in the carriage house."

I won't stay on this place a minute longer than I have to! Nat thought.

It was as though he had spoken aloud, for George gave the boy a knowing look. "Remember what I told you earlier: Don't trust anyone."

"Is that why you didn't stop and talk to any of the others we saw just now?"

"Can't never tell which one's a spy for the master or mistress. Most of the time it's one of the house slaves that gives you away, but you can't really tell until it's too late. That's why some poor slave got caught trying to run away. Some even try putting pepper on their feet so's the dogs can't track them, but I don't know of anyone who made that work."

"Why're you telling me this again?"

George raised gray eyebrows. "I've got the best job on the whole plantation," he said proudly, then paused.

For a moment, Nat thought George had changed the subject, but George took a deep breath and continued.

"I'm the only one who can be off the place and not be

★ ★

caught by the white patrollers who love to catch one of us without a pass so they can beat up on us. I get to drive the master
to other plantations where other drivers are waiting, same as
me. I get to drive into the village and other places most slaves
never do. I meet other drivers. We talk. We listen. Sometimes
we know things before the white folks do."

Not sure he trusted the old slave, Nat cautiously asked,
"Have you been to Glenbury Hill, where I used to live?"

"Many times. I knew Hector, the driver there before the
master died. Thaddeus Whitman was a good master. Didn't beat
a body half to death for no good reason. He never sold nobody
'down the river,' neither."

Down the river!

An involuntary shiver rippled over Nat's body, raising
gooseflesh that prickled. Every slave knew that being sold into
the deep South meant a one-way trip down the mighty Mississippi. It was impossible to escape from there to a free state.
Virginia was close to freedom—but even that was not an easy
journey.

Nat's eyes automatically turned skyward for the one guiding light that had helped a few slaves to freedom.

George laughed softly but without humor. "Can't see the
North Star this time of day, Nat."

"I wasn't looking for that," he exclaimed hastily, again having that uneasy feeling that George could read his mind.

" 'Course not," George agreed. "Well, we better get you
back inside before your young master comes home. Just be
careful with him. He's got a mean streak, 'specially when it
comes to laying the leather on one of us."

"I'll remember," Nat replied, secretly determining that he
would hide his feelings and plans until the right time. Mean-
while, he would trust no one, not even George. Or was it possible that the old slave had an uncanny ability to discern even
what went on in Nat's mind?

★ ★

★ ★ ★ ★ ★

At dusk, a house servant instructed Nat in lighting candles and starting a cheery blaze in the fireplace of Briarstone's south drawing room. Then, silent as shadows, the slave called Jason and the teenage boy discreetly withdrew but stayed in the great hallway in case they were needed quickly.

Emily joined Julie and her mother in listening to the war news from Uncle Silas and William. Out of the corner of her eye, Emily could see Nat. He was close enough to hear every word the white folks would say in the drawing room. However, Emily had already learned that the master and mistress spoke as freely in front of their servants as they would with a piece of furniture.

Her uncle settled himself in a comfortable chair nearest the fireplace and cleared his throat. "It's the consensus of knowledgeable men in the village," he began, "that we're too far south of Washington and too far west and inland to be prime targets for any Federal invasion."

Emily and Julie exchanged relieved glances.

William added quickly, "But that doesn't mean we can forget the danger. We have to prepare, just in case."

"Does that mean the girls and I have to flee?" Aunt Anna asked anxiously. "If so, where would we go?"

Emily fearfully awaited her uncle's answer. Like many Virginia planters, he was involved in politics, which often kept him away from home for extended periods. Julie had confided to Emily that her father secretly hoped to rise to some high office. Before the Union began to interfere in Southern politics, Julie had heard that he might someday become the eighth president from Virginia.

"No one knows," Uncle Silas replied soberly. "Only six states have seceded so far: Mississippi, Florida, Alabama, Georgia, Louisiana, and Texas. The four border states of Maryland, Delaware, Kentucky, and Missouri could still go either way. Virginia will join the Confederacy, and probably five others."

William broke in. "At a minimum, that will be eleven states and maybe fifteen against the Union ones. But today everyone agreed that one Southerner is worth three Yankee soldiers."

"That's brave talk," his father said. "I expect us to win, but I don't agree with some of our friends that this will be a short war. There's no telling what might happen if it drags on for a year or more."

Emily's thoughts leaped to her former Illinois home and her best friend's older brother. Brice Barlow was about eighteen, so he would have to join up. He had often unmercifully teased Jessie, his sister, and Emily. She hated to think of him getting wounded or killed.

"So," Uncle Silas continued, "we're going to instruct the servants where and how to hide our food and household valuables in the woods, just in case. Anna, have the servants pack a trunk full of your personal possessions. Do the same for the girls. George will have a carriage ready for instant flight if necessary. We will develop alternate plans on where you will all be safe."

"But I don't want to leave here!" Julie protested.

"Nobody does," her brother replied bluntly. "But we can't trust that scoundrel Lincoln. Right, Papa?"

His father nodded. "He's talking about holding the Union together, but that's not what rouses people emotionally. In a war, you've got to stir people up in order for them to support their male family members and friends dying or getting wounded. That issue is slavery."

"The Northern abolitionists have already whipped that up, and it'll get worse," William added quickly.

"Unfortunately, that's true," his father agreed. "Slavery will become the burning emotional cause for which the Union will shed their own men's blood. But without the slavery system, the South's way of life will be ruined. That's true both socially and from an agricultural point of view. So we have no choice

★ ★

but to defend that system with our own blood."

Without thinking, Emily blurted, "Uncle Silas, I think you and William are being unfair to Mr. Lincoln."

"You're speaking out of turn!" William snapped.

A warm flush swept over Emily. "Don't I have a right to express an opinion?"

She felt Julie's warning squeeze on her arm and caught the disapproving look by her aunt, but Emily did not back down. She steadily met her uncle's cold eyes.

"You are my late brother's only surviving child," he said coldly. "It is our Christian duty to take you into our home, but a little respect is expected in return."

"I didn't mean any disrespect," Emily protested, "but in our home, everyone was allowed to express an opinion, even if it wasn't popular. That's all I did just now."

William glowered at her. "You've had your say, but this is not your concern."

Her eyes opened wide in surprise. "It's not my concern that a war is starting, so Aunt Anna and Cousin Julie and I might have to leave for who-knows-where?"

"If invaders come," Uncle Silas said in the same disapproving tone, "they will be wearing Federal uniforms. They will come as thieves, robbers, and killers to attack our people, who only want to be left alone."

"I know countless men and boys in Illinois," Emily fired back, fighting to control her anger. "They are all gentlemen. They're not thieves and killers!"

William hooted loudly at that. "When they put on a uniform and invade where the home folks can't see what they do, those 'gentlemen' will do worse than Papa said. Mark my words, Emily!"

She bit her tongue to stop the hot retort that leaped to her lips. With great effort, she pushed back her chair and stood up. "I would like to be excused."

"Shall I come with you?" Julie asked.

★ ★

Hesitating, Emily took a deep breath and scanned the icy faces of William and her uncle. A quick shift to Aunt Anna's face showed she had lowered her eyes. Emily was sure that was a sign that she agreed with her husband and son. But if Julie walked out, she might get in trouble.

"Thanks," Emily replied, "but I need to be alone."

She hurried up the wide stairs to the second-story bed-chamber next to Julie's. *I want to be alone so I can figure out how to get back to Illinois. Jessie and her mother will take me in—if I can just get there before things here blow up in my face!*

WAITING FOR TROUBLE

Two days after the firing on Fort Sumter, Gideon quietly dressed for church in the tiny bedroom he shared with Isham and Ben. There was barely room to move between the three built-in pole bunks and the handmade chest of drawers, so Ben had already finished and gone to wait in the kitchen.

Standing beside Isham, Gideon finished parting his long hair on the left and rolling it over to the right so it would be neat enough to suit his mother.

His older half brother asked, "Why so quiet, Gid?"

He hesitated to answer. He felt proud of Isham volunteering to go fight Yankees, yet he hated having to add Isham's chores to the ones already on his shoulders. Most of all, he resented having to postpone his own secret dream of being a writer.

"How long do you think you'll be gone?" he asked, turning to lift baggy dress pants from their horizontal pole fastened to the wall over his bed.

Isham shrugged. "Who knows?"

"I hope it won't be long."

"You mad at me for going away, Gid?"

Gideon tried to avoid a direct answer. "It's not your fault. It's those Yankees."

Isham turned from the mirror to look directly at Gideon. "You're different from Ben. You go off alone a lot, even when it makes Papa mad. Sometimes you talk, but you never seem to say what's really on your mind."

Gideon pulled on the baggy pants, which were made too big so he wouldn't quickly outgrow them. "No matter what I do, there's no pleasing Papa," he explained with a hint of bitterness. "So I go off alone to stay out of his way and to think."

"About what?"

A shrug was Gideon's only reply as he pulled on shoes he had outgrown because there was no money to replace them.

Isham knelt in front of Gideon to ask, "Don't you trust me?"

"It's not that. I just don't think you'd understand."

"Why not?"

"You'd laugh."

"No, I wouldn't. Look, I'm going away to the war, so don't you want to tell me what's on your mind before I go?"

Gideon considered that for a long moment before nodding. "All right, if you promise not to tell anyone."

"I promise."

Taking a deep breath, Gideon tried to put his deepest emotions into words. "I walk through the woods or down to the swamp where it's peaceful and quiet. I look at the sky and the trees and birds and animals and feel something deep down inside. I want to write about those things, but I don't have the words. That's the trouble: I feel so many things, but I don't know how to put them down on paper."

"Then how do you plan to become a writer?"

"I don't know. There's nobody to ask, but I thought of going to someplace like New York to write books."

"Books? What kind of books?"

"Well, stories . . . like *Uncle Tom's Cabin*."

"You read that Yankee woman's pack of lies about slavery?"

"I found it behind a store in the village where somebody probably threw it away."

Isham whistled in surprise. "Does Papa know?"

"No, nor Mama, neither. But I knew a long time ago when

she read Bible stories to us that I wanted to write. Only I don't know how."

"So that's why you go to that plantation school even though William sometimes beats up on you and Papa thinks it's a waste of time?"

"Partly that and partly because I hate farming."

Isham sat down on the narrow bed and dropped a big-brotherly arm over Gideon's shoulders. "When I go to the war, you have my chores to do as well as your own, so it looks to you like you'll never get to be a writer. Is that right?"

Gideon nodded, grateful that Isham hadn't laughed and was even understanding.

"Why can't you write your stories here, instead of going off someplace?"

"There's nothing to write about here."

"Are you sure? I bet you could find all kinds of stories hereabout if you tried. Think what you've seen or heard lately that you could write about."

"Such as. . . ?"

"Well, the war starting and how that's going to affect you and all of us. Why, even the slaves and those nasty Lodges."

"I don't know. . . ." Gideon began doubtfully, but Isham quickly broke in.

"If nothing else, you could write about what it's like to grow up in a war. Why, there's never been a war like this one where brothers and fathers and sons are going to be divided and maybe kill each other in battle. You could keep a diary about that."

Scornfully, Gideon said, "Only girls keep diaries."

"Then keep a man's journal. You think about all this later— now we'd better get started for church. I'm anxious to hear what the preacher's going to say today."

Emily's spirits had somewhat revived the next morning when she and Julie boarded the Lodge family's town coach with George the driver. Aunt Anna was already seated inside facing them, so the girls had to ride backward. William and his father were to follow in a separate, smaller carriage to test Nat's driving ability. Riding along the public road that led away from Briarstone, Julie chattered away about how pretty the sky was and how the tobacco plants were growing.

Abruptly, she turned to Emily. "It's hard to believe there's a war starting," she said, lightly touching her curls, which her black maid had helped her create.

"It's very unreal," Emily agreed. Her golden hair hung in waterfall style over her left shoulder. She had personally rolled the front hair over a cushion because she wasn't used to having a maid assist her.

Aunt Anna pointed out the side window. "Here come those despicable Tugwells in their dirty old wagon. Oh my! I do believe we're all going to come to the crossroad at the same time."

Emily leaned forward to see if the boy she had met at the slave auction was in the wagon. A woman and three children sat on seats made of bales of hay placed against the sides of the wagon bed. Their Sunday "go-to-meeting" clothes were protected by an old horse blanket. Two males sat on the high front seat, with the taller one driving. It took a moment for Emily to realize one of them was Gideon.

Aunt Anna clucked disapprovingly. "I hope they're going to give way before we all turn onto the turnpike. My dress will be ruined if they raise dust by going ahead of us all the way into the village."

Julie said confidently, "Papa and William will be along shortly. They'll run them off the road if that wagon dares do that."

Emily watched apprehensively as the approaching brown mule kept up a slow but steady pace that was about to put the wagon into the intersection moments ahead of the coach.

"George!" Aunt Anna called through the window while thumping on the roof with the point of her parasol, "Go faster! Beat that farmer to the intersection!"

Emily heard the reinsman call to the span of horses, and the coach lurched ahead. Glancing again at the wagon, she saw the tall, young man sitting beside Gideon snap the reins over the mule's back, urging him to go faster.

Aunt Anna exclaimed, "What utter disregard for their betters! They're going to try beating us!"

Emily knew from previous conversations that Uncle Silas was determined to buy the Tugwells' river-bottom land or run them out of the country. In spite of herself, Emily silently urged the other driver on.

"Oh!" Aunt Anna stormed as the mule drew steadily ahead. "They're actually going to race us there. Oh my! How I wish my husband was close enough to see this!"

Emily and her cousin stuck their heads out of the window to see better. The Tugwell driver reached the intersection at a fast clip and swung onto the turnpike so fast that the wagon wheels slipped to the side, throwing up a cloud of dust.

George called "Whoa!" to the matched carriage team, slowing to avoid a collision. The three passengers grabbed on to the nearest window or doorpost to keep from being thrown out of their seats while the dust obscured the other vehicle.

Julie quickly recovered her balance and again thrust her head out the window. "Look! What're they doing now?"

Emily stuck her face up beside her cousin's to see better. Instead of continuing on the roadway, the young driver guided the mule off to the right shoulder. The mule obediently stopped when the driver pulled back on the reins.

The Lodge coach lurched ahead and quickly drew beside the wagon. Mrs. Tugwell clutched her bonnet with one hand and the youngest of the three children with the other hand. All stared at the fine carriage. The Tugwell driver smiled broadly,

★ ★

lifted his hat in a gallant gesture, and gave a slight bow.

"Ladies!" he said, replacing his hat to make a sweeping motion for them to go ahead. "After you."

Emily smiled at the driver, who jabbed an elbow into Gideon's ribs. For a moment he seemed to hesitate, then he looked directly at Emily before waving and smiling at her.

As the coach speeded up again, Aunt Anna stormed, "Did you see that? They mocked us! Oh, wait till I tell my husband about this!"

Emily and Julie looked at each other, then quickly hid giggles behind their hands.

Nearing the village outskirts, Gideon cocked his head to better hear shouting and a drum thumping ahead of them from the town commons. "What's that?" he asked Isham.

He guided the mule around the smoldering remains of a bonfire built in the center of the roadway. "Must have been from last night," Isham explained. "It was so bright I saw the horizon lit up and thought at first the whole place was on fire. Then I could hear, ever so faintly, the drums and brass musical instruments. Now the bands are so loud I can barely make myself heard."

"People are celebrating the start of war?" Gideon's voice shot up in surprise.

"Not really celebrating, little brother. They're mostly letting off steam, whipping up a patriotic fervor to encourage men like me to enlist. They're also trying to impress all the pretty women. I'll do that when I sign up after church."

It was a stirring sight with old men and women, little children, and others unable to fight who turned out to honor those who would defend their land and way of life from the threatening Federals.

It was better than any Fourth-of-July parade he had ever seen before the trouble started with the North. But Gideon's gaze was drawn from the frenzied crowds and marching bands to the Lodges' carriage when it turned off toward the stately brick church with stained-glass windows and its tall steeple pointing skyward.

Isham carefully guided the Tugwell mule through the throngs and continued through the village to the white frame church with its simple cross as plain as the rest of the building. The back lot was already filled with other wagons, a few buckboards, a couple of shays, and a black buggy. Several people headed toward the Tugwell wagon as Gideon stepped down onto the front wheel and tied the mule to a long hitching rail.

He took one quick look back toward the other church spire and remembered how the girl with the golden hair had smiled at him.

The moment George pulled the coach into the back of the line of the other plantation owners' carriages, a slender, well-dressed man in his thirties hurried toward the Lodges' vehicle.

Emily, sitting nearest the door, thought he was coming to open it for her, so she waited.

Julie whispered, "That's Oliver Fitzhugh, a traveling temperance lecturer. He's been here for a month or so."

Striding purposefully up to the coach, Fitzhugh thrust his beardless face close to the small open window in the door. Ignoring the girls, he spoke without greeting Mrs. Lodge.

"Where's your husband?"

"He's coming with our son. Why? Something wrong?"

"Depends. Have you heard the news?" he asked. Without waiting for a reply, he continued. "The Union forces surrendered today at Fort Sumter! It's now in our hands. It's a great victory, but that tyrant in Washington won't stand for that. He'll send Federal troops to take it back, so the war just got hotter!"

Emily closed her eyes in pain and heard her aunt's sudden gasp of horror. To the temperance lecturer, the Confederacy

★ ★

had won a great victory, but to the girl, it was the start of something terrible.

In two days shots fired away down in Charleston Harbor were being heard in Church Falls. Soon they might be heard all over the South, and older boys she had known as a little girl in Virginia or more recently in Illinois would soon be suffering wounds or even death.

Julie whispered, "You all right, Emily?"

Nodding, Emily opened her eyes.

"Then please step out so Mama and I can, too."

"Excuse me." Emily bent to step through the door that George had opened. The soles of her dress shoes had barely touched the ground when a shout from the street made her turn to look that way.

Several men ran with a stout pole on which a disheveled man bounced along in the center. He vainly tried to ease the agony of straddling the narrow pole.

Emily turned away from the sight to ask, "Aunt Anna, what're they doing to that poor man?"

"Riding him out of town on a rail," she explained. Turning to Fitzhugh, she asked, "I wonder what he did?"

"I've seen him around. He says he's a traveling tradesman, but I've heard rumors that he's a Union spy."

"Spy?" Emily and Julie exclaimed together.

Fitzhugh nodded solemnly. "A traitor to our noble cause, don't you agree, Mrs. Lodge?"

"Oh yes, indeed. Why, when my father last visited, he told my husband and me that there will be spies on both sides of this war. My father was nearly forty when he served in the suppression of Sac and Fox Indians under Black Hawk back in 1832. Since then, my father has been interested in military campaigns, so he's read about such matters. He knows a great deal about the Revolution."

"But, Mama," Julie protested while the cries of the sus-

★ ★

pected traitor faded as he was lost to sight among some buildings. "Spies in Church Falls?"

"I believe your grandfather, and so does your father. That's why I meant to warn you girls about being discreet with what you say or do from now on."

Emily glanced at the temperance speaker, who nodded.

"Listen to her, girls. You shouldn't trust anyone, even here in this peaceful country town."

Emily and Julie looked at each other, disbelief showing in their eyes. But they fell silent and followed Mrs. Lodge and Fitzhugh toward the church.

Emily found it hard to believe there would be spies here, but she knew for sure that the Union and the newly formed seven states in the Confederate States of America were now locked into a war that nobody really wanted.

What would happen if it came there? What would happen to her only living relatives? What would happen to Gideon and his family? And what would happen to her?

With a sigh, Emily mounted the steps into the church, knowing that all she could do was wait and pray that the war would never come there.

YANKEE
SOLDIERS
COMING!

Back at Briarstone after church, Emily and Julie had changed clothes and were now in Emily's second-story bedroom. She stood before the mirror and started to pick up the hairbrush, but the teenage black girl who had been assigned as her personal maid also reached for the brush. "Thank you, Lizzie," Emily said with a smile, "but I would rather do this myself."

"Yes'm, Miz Emily," the girl replied with an uneasy glance toward Julie to see if she approved.

Julie nodded and motioned to her own maid. "Toby, I think I'll do the same. You two may wait downstairs. We'll be down in a minute."

When the maids had closed the door after them, Julie observed, "You've been very quiet ever since church. Is something wrong?"

"No, no, I'm just thinking."

"What about? Those Tugwells racing us to the crossroads and then acting so superior?"

"No, I was thinking about my family." Emily's eyes suddenly misted. "I miss them so very much."

"I'm sure you do, but you've got us."

Emily tried to blink back the mist and force a smile. "I'm grateful for that, but sometimes I get so lonesome I could die."

"Please don't say that! I know it's hard on you, losing

★ ★

everybody in so short a time, but you mean so very much to me."

"You mean a lot to me, too, Julie, but I miss my best friend in Illinois and all the familiar places of home." Emily's voice cracked.

"This is your home now, and I want to be your best friend, the same as Jessie Barlow was in Illinois."

"Oh, you are, Julie! I feel so loved by you, and . . . well, this is a beautiful place, but it's not mine."

"I understand how you feel, because although it's where I was born, it's really my father's and brother's place. They both get on their high horses and boss me around as if I were one of the servants."

Sighing, Julie continued. "And my poor mother—always feeling poorly and afraid to speak her mind. I don't even think she's happy here. So having you live with us makes it bearable for me. I can hardly wait until I'm fifteen or sixteen so I can get married and move away from here."

"That's no reason to get married."

"Lots of girls marry when they're fifteen. My mother was sixteen. She lost two babies before William and I came along." Julie's thoughts followed that sad turn. "Why, I've heard that the average Southern white woman loses at least one child before it's six years old."

Emily didn't reply because the discussion seemed to reopen her own wounds from the recent loss of her family.

Julie sighed and continued. "So many women die young. My grandpa told me about a woman who lived on the other side of Church Falls. She married at fifteen and had ten children by the time she died at age twenty-seven."

Emily broke in to end the morbid conversation. "I smell the food being brought into the dining room. Shouldn't we go to the table?"

"I guess so." Julie started to open the bedchamber door, then stopped. "I know you feel strongly about the Union, but

★ ★

please be careful what you say in front of my father and brother when we're at dinner."

"I'll try," Emily promised and followed her cousin down the curving stairs.

★ ★ ★ ★ ★

Sundays traditionally meant that slaves were given time off from their plantation chores, although the house servants rarely enjoyed that privilege. However, as dusk settled across Briarstone, William told Nat he could join the others in the slave quarters.

Nat went to the carriage house, where Uncle George was sitting outside the wide doors smoking his homemade pipe.

"I'm glad to see you," the old slave remarked. "I was just thinking of taking a walk to get the kinks out of these old bones. You want to come along?"

"I'd like that."

George led the way past the neat English box hedges around the big house toward the back where the cabins stood. They were similar to what Nat had known at Glenbury Plantation but not as well made.

Most were makeshift one-room, windowless structures about sixteen by eighteen feet. The slaves had built the cabins with a simple door, and a fireplace and chimney. These had floors, although George said some he had seen were set right on the ground. Sleep was on mattresses made of corn shucks. The furnishings were simple: a crude table, a chair or two, and some pots, pans, and bowls.

George led the way past small vegetable gardens, which slaves tended in their spare time. There wasn't much of that because the cow horn awakened them daily around four so they could be in the fields by dawn. They worked until it was too dark to see. Then, weary beyond words in body and spirit, the field hands returned to their cabins, made their suppers, and did other chores.

★ ★

George slowed before a cabin with smoke curling from the fireplace chimney and fresh green sprouts indicating a flower garden had been started. He told Nat, "I've got somebody I want you to meet."

Rounding the cabin from the side, Nat saw a teenage girl with skin as light as his own gently washing the back of a middle-aged black man who was smoking a pipe.

"Sarah," George said, approaching the couple, "this is young Master William's new body servant, Nat."

The girl was about fourteen, Nat guessed, and well on her way to being a pretty woman. A heavy iron ring encircled her right ankle. It had rubbed the skin until it was red and swollen. She nodded to Nat but didn't speak before returning to tending the man's back.

George introduced the seated man as Pete. He also nodded without speaking, then continued smoking.

Nat was attracted to the girl's delicate features, but she ignored him, so he stared at the man's bare back.

Only once before had Nat seen what fearful damage a leather strap could do to human flesh. He had heard about slaves being whipped to death, but the victim before him had obviously survived what could have been a deadly whipping. Pete's back was an unending network of long scars extending from just below his neck to his waist. The skin had been raised a fraction of an inch where the blows had healed in ridged furrows.

George explained quietly, "Pete and Sarah ran away about a year ago. The master hired a slave catcher named Barley Cobb to run them down with his bloodhounds. They nearly tore Pete up before he was brought back here and this was done to him. The girl was whipped, but not so hard. She has to wear a shackle so it's harder to run."

It took willpower for Nat to take his eyes off the sight before him. But he managed to look at George and again saw some-

★ ★

thing in his eyes that made Nat aware that he was being warned about trying to escape.

"Cobb still lives around here," George said after saying good-bye to the two slaves. "He has mighty mean dogs, and he's as mean as they are."

Nat didn't reply but looked back at the couple in front of the cabin.

"Remember what I told you before," George said quietly. "Don't trust anyone . . . with anything."

This time Nat responded, "Thanks."

They walked back to the carriage house in silence while Nat thought about how impossible his goal seemed. But slowly he felt his determination growing stronger. He would escape to freedom and then somehow find and lead his mother and siblings to freedom, too. He tried not to think of the price of failure.

★　★　★　★　★

Everyone was solemn at the Tugwells' after returning from church. Isham had enjoyed the unusual attention from all the women before he proudly walked down to where a local company of militia was forming. He had signed his name with a flourish, then everyone said good-bye to him. The rest of his family had returned home in thoughtful silence. Nobody said it aloud, but each wondered if they would ever see him alive again.

Gideon looked at his mother as she salted three cut-up squirrels for frying. Her nose was slowly turning red, a sure indication to Gideon that she was silently crying over Isham. It hurt Gideon to see tears forming in his mother's eyes, so he turned away to watch Kate preparing the cast-iron skillet for making brown gravy.

Ben turned from where he had been looking out the kitchen window. "How much longer, Mama?" he asked.

"Soon." Her answer was short. "Why don't you and Gideon

★　★

find a verse to read before the blessing?"

"Ah, Mama, I don't feel like it."

Old Gideon spoke, his voice unusually low. "Better do as she says, Benjamin. Gideon, reach the Book down off that shelf."

As Gideon did so, Ben complained, "Mama, I bet as soon as you start frying that squirrel, Barley Cobb will smell it and come straight here to get a share."

Gideon smiled, knowing there was some truth to that. The slave catcher had a bad habit of unexpectedly showing up at mealtimes. The Tugwells never had much, but out of Christian charity, they invited Cobb to join them. He always had, eating so much that the Tugwells had to take smaller portions to make sure the guest had enough.

Sitting side by side on the plank bench in front of the table, Gideon and Ben thumbed through the Bible for a verse suitable for a brother gone off to war.

The words began to blur on the page, and Gideon's thoughts drifted back to what Isham had said about staying home and writing. *Maybe*, Gideon thought, still leafing through the familiar stories in the Scriptures, *maybe there is something I could write about. But what?*

Suddenly, the Tugwells' two hounds barked loudly and charged out from under the high porch.

Ben exclaimed, "I bet that's Barley Cobb!"

"Benjamin," his mother scolded gently. "Be nice!"

"He's not, so why should I be?" Ben said under his breath so only Gideon could hear. Gideon hid a smile behind his hand, closed the Bible, and headed toward the door.

He opened it to see an unshaven, uncouth, fortyish, tobacco-chewing "bummer." He had been twice widowed and was childless.

"Well, howdy, Gideon," Cobb said heartily. "I was passing by the swamp and realized it wouldn't be neighborly if'n I was to jist pass by without stoppin' to visit a spell."

★ ★

Gideon was almost sure he heard Benjamin make a choking sound, but the boys' mother hurried over. Wiping her hands on her apron, she invited the man in.

"Thankee kindly, Miz Tugwell," he said through a tobacco-stained wild brown beard. He removed a battered old brown slouch hat, which allowed uncombed, shoulder-length brown hair to spill down in back and on both sides of his head. He stomped noisily across the wooden floor in military boots. They were wrinkled at the ankles and had tops extending almost to his knees.

"Will you have time to join us at the table?" Mrs. Tugwell asked.

Gideon, following Cobb across the floor, already knew the answer to that. He sent a warning look to Ben, who made another sound as though he were gagging on something.

"Well, now, I reckon I will." Cobb shook hands with Mr. Tugwell, adding, "Say, you might be interested to know about somethin' I seen down by the woods."

He explained, "I seen some fresh horse tracks in the dust. Now, I don't aim to scare nobody, but I'm purty sure them was made by Union cavalry horses!"

The announcement brought startled exclamations from everyone except little Lilly, who didn't know what it meant.

Mr. Tugwell asked soberly, "You sure? There have been no reports of any Federals in Virginia yet."

"Nearly positive." Cobb looked around at the anxious faces. "They might be scouts, you know, slipping along like weasels to spy out the land before the main force comes in behind them."

"Mercy!" Gideon's mother exclaimed, turning to her husband. "Do you suppose they'll come here?"

"Might not," Cobb replied before Mr. Tugwell could. "You bein' back off the public road and all, down here in the river bottom under all these trees. And with the swamp guarding you on one side . . ."

★ ★

He left his thought unfinished before adding quickly, "Still, it might be best if you hid all you got that them no-count Yankees could carry off. Any money you got tucked away, the meat in your smokehouse—"

"I suppose you'd be willing to help, Cobb?" Mr. Tugwell interrupted.

"Well, now that you mention it, it would be the neighborly thing to do. . . ."

"I'm obliged," Mr. Tugwell said, "but I think my family and I can manage alone. Martha, you about to put food on the table?"

When she nodded, Gideon realized he had been holding his breath. He didn't trust Barley Cobb; didn't trust him as far as he could throw the old brown mule. Neither, it seemed, did his father.

When they all sat down at the table, Gideon wondered if maybe Isham was right. Maybe there was something worth writing about around here after all.

★   ★   ★   ★   ★

For the first time in weeks, Gideon wasn't needed on the farm, so the next morning he dressed to walk to school with Ben and Kate. Their father cautioned them not to say anything about Cobb's story of seeing horse tracks possibly made by Union horseshoes. Mr. Tugwell didn't say so, but it was apparent that he didn't believe the slave catcher.

Most plantation families taught the children at home, bringing in tutors for music, geography, and other specialized subjects. Silas Lodge had built the white frame school because he had finally found a good, dependable overseer in Lewis Toombs. His six children, including Edwin, tended to keep him in one place, so the schoolhouse had been another incentive to continue working at Briarstone.

Nearing the school grounds from the backside, Ben and Kate dashed off to visit with friends before the bell rang. Gideon walked past some boys playing "ante over" by throwing a ball over the low school roof. Gideon glanced about, wondering if Emily was around.

Rounding the corner near the flagpole and the front door, Gideon stopped short.

William Lodge was reaching for the dangling overhead rope under the small open tower. Ringing the bell was a privilege granted by Mr. Boswell, the teacher. William dropped his hands and scowled at Gideon.

"Where do you think you're going?" William demanded.

"To class." Gideon felt his skin pucker, remembering past beatings the older, heavier boy had inflicted on him. Hastily, Gideon added, "Mr. Boswell lets me come when I can get time off from the farm."

William haughtily replied, "My father hired Boswell to teach decent white people, not the likes of you." His voice rose, causing other students nearby to look.

To avoid making William any more angry, Gideon did not reply but started to walk around him.

"Besides," William added, stepping to block the way, "yesterday you forgot your place by racing to cut off my mother and the girls with that stupid mule of yours."

"It wasn't a race." Gideon didn't see any use in saying he wasn't driving yesterday. "We let them go by even though we got there first."

"Don't argue with me! From now on, only the overseer's children and my family can go to this school. No white trash dirt farmer or his family can smell up the place, so you take your little brother and sister and run before you get seriously hurt!"

Gideon hesitated while other children, including Edwin Toombs, crowded around, attracted by William's rising voice. Emily and Julie came out of the schoolroom and stopped in the open doorway. That embarrassed Gideon to again be

★ ★

humiliated in their presence—especially Emily's. He hoped she wouldn't say anything.

Emily spoke quickly. "Please, William, let him in."

Whirling around to face her, William yelled, "Didn't you learn anything before? Mind your own business!"

Gideon's embarrassment deepened as the teacher came striding out of the schoolroom. He was a stubby man in his twenties, with a black mustache and a widow's peak. "What's going on here?"

William explained, "I don't want him or his family sitting in the same room with decent folks."

Frowning, Boswell replied, "I have your father's permission for Gideon and his siblings to be here."

"You let this dirt farmer in today, and I'll have my father discharge you!" William threatened.

Boswell's face darkened in a manner Gideon had seen once before directed at Edwin Toombs, who had back-talked.

"William, you may do as you wish with your father, but I am in charge here! Gideon stays, and so do—"

He broke off and glanced down the dirt road leading up to the schoolhouse. Nat was drumming his heels into a horse's flanks, leaning over the saddle and riding fast.

"Something's wrong!" Julie cried.

All the students ran toward the school steps as the slave boy drew rein before his young master.

"You'd better have a good excuse for running that horse so hard!" William yelled.

Nat slid off the horse flecked with foam. "I have. Mistress sent me to warn everyone: Yankees are headed this way!"

STARS AND BARS

The cousins ran hard, with Julie making little sobbing sounds of fright between gasps for air. Emily wasn't so concerned about Yankee soldiers. She did fret about the thought of having to quickly pack her few belongings in a carpetbag for a fast escape.

They reached Briarstone out of breath, glad they had not seen any uniforms. With safety in sight, they slowed slightly. They ignored the tree-shaded lane and cut across the wide expanse of lawn toward the solid-looking big house with its stately Corinthian columns.

"I don't see the servants running about, hiding silverware and other valuables in the woods," Julie puffed. "No one is dragging trunks out to be loaded onto carriages."

"Neither do I," Emily replied. "But there's your mother by the front door."

"False alarm!" Aunt Anna called. "It was just a rumor!"

"What?" Julie asked, panting up to stop in front of her mother. "Are you sure?"

"Your father just rode in after confirming that the so-called Yankee soldiers were really some of our boys in blue uniforms."

"Confederates in *blue*?" Emily asked in surprise.

"Yes." Aunt Anna made a clucking sound of disapproval. "I do wish that both armies would agree on which color uniforms each is going to wear. The way it is, a body can't tell for sure which is which."

"I guess that's because the Confederates say a soldier has to supply his own uniform," Emily said.

"Nobody's really organized for war," Aunt Anna commented sadly. "After a while, I'm sure President Davis and his cabinet will issue standard uniforms and equipment." She turned toward the front door when it opened, and her personal maid appeared with something rolled on the end of a three-foot-long stick.

"Oh, girls," Aunt Anna said, taking the object from the servant, "look what my husband bought in the village this morning. It's our new Confederate flag."

Emily and Julie exchanged relieved looks, then smiled and began catching their breaths as the flag was unrolled from the staff. It had three wide stripes: a red one at the top, a white one in the middle, and another red one at the bottom. The latter ran the entire length of the flag, but the other two stripes were shorter because they fitted up against the blue field at the upper, inner corner. Seven white stars in a circle there represented the original seceded states.

"It's called the Stars and Bars," Aunt Anna explained. "Isn't it beautiful?"

Emily didn't answer, but Julie observed, "It looks a little like the regular American—I mean, Union flag."

"I suppose it does somewhat," Aunt Anna admitted. "Oh well, I'm having the servants mount it where everyone can see where we stand in this awful war. I think it will look best on this column. Julie, would you hold it up there, then both of you give me your opinions."

Emily involuntarily turned away, suddenly very emotional over the thought that the familiar star-spangled banner she had known all her life no longer represented all the American people.

She was just in time to see a runabout turn off the road

★ ★

into the long, tree-lined lane leading to the big house. The open, one-seated vehicle was very popular, although it resembled a piano box on wheels.

Aunt Anna said, "That's George returning from the village. I sent him for the mail." She sighed heavily. "I heard that the Union's postmaster general has decided there will be no more mail to the Confederate states after May thirty-first."

"Oh no!" Emily exclaimed in dismay. "That means I can't write my friend Jessie anymore!"

That knowledge sent a surge of sadness through Emily. No more mail! What an awful thought.

George reined in the horse, tipped his hat, and handed a bundle of letters to the mistress. She took them, leafed through, and handed a letter to Emily. "Speaking of your Illinois friend, here's one from her."

"Thank you." Emily looked at the familiar handwriting. "If you'll excuse me," she said to her aunt, "I'll read it in the bedchamber."

"Share it with me," Julie urged.

The cousins hurried inside the big house with the sound of the new Confederate flag gently snapping in the breeze behind them.

★ ★ ★ ★ ★

Gideon followed the brown mule down the furrow, but his mind was elsewhere. He was vaguely aware of smelling the freshly turned earth and hearing birds calling behind him as they squabbled over worms and insects suddenly exposed to sunlight.

It was common for the boy to daydream as he went about the hated farm work. The result was often careless work and angry reproof from his father, but Gideon had learned to escape into faraway thoughts.

This morning he reviewed what Isham had said about finding things to write about at home. Stories, Gideon had already learned, were mostly about people. Barley Cobb was an interesting person, Gideon thought. Maybe a story could be written about him. Or Nat, the mulatto slave boy, or even Emily, the Yankee girl living with Confederate relatives here in Virginia. But what kind of a story?

His father's voice jerked him back to reality. "That's the crookedest furrow I ever saw in my life!"

Mr. Tugwell came striding angrily across the uneven ground. "Can't you do a simple thing like plowing straight?" he demanded. "Even Ben can do better than that!"

Blowing his breath out in tired resignation, Gideon stopped the mule to wait for his father. What he had said about Ben was true, even though he was still so little he had to stand between the plow handles instead of walking behind them and holding them in calloused hands.

Mr. Tugwell glared down at Gideon, then turned to look back at the new furrow. It rippled from side to side like a snake curving across an open field. "You'd better let me finish this. You can chop firewood."

Unwilling to speak for fear of bringing more of his father's ire down on him, Gideon released the plow handles made smooth and glistening from countless hours of being gripped by sweating hands.

"Just a minute," his father said as the boy turned away. "I've been thinking that with all this war scare, we had better get our summer wheat crop ready for market. Otherwise, if fighting breaks out before we get this on the train, we may not have any cash for the rest of the year."

Hope made Gideon's face light up. "When are we going?"

"Not 'we,' just me."

Gideon's features faded into disappointment. "But I went last year!"

"That was when Isham was here to take care of things until we got back. I'll have to go alone this time."

"But one man can't handle our big wagon all loaded down,

★ ★

plus two mules—and we've only got one now!"

"I got no choice, Gideon. I've been thinking about how we can borrow another mule to make a team. The load will be too heavy for Napoleon alone. Much as I hate to be obligated, maybe Barley Cobb will loan me his mule."

"Don't do it, Papa! If you do, he'll be here every day to get a free meal. Besides, his mule is the most ornery, cantankerous biter and kicker I ever saw!"

"I may not have a choice. Now, you get on that wood, and I'll try to straighten out this mess you've made."

Gideon watched his father loop the continuous leather line across his shoulders so his hands could be free to hold the plow handle. He clucked to Napoleon, and the plow bit into the earth, leaving a neat, straight furrow behind.

For another moment Gideon stood, his mind suddenly busy with a new thought. *I've got to go to market with Papa! I want to see Manassas Junction again and watch the trains. I've just got to—but how?*

The market trip was weeks away. Maybe he could think of something between now and then.

★ ★ ★ ★ ★

Julie lay face down on her high bed with its lace canopy, while Emily sat by the window and tore open her friend's letter. A sheet fell out on the floor. Emily reached for it just as a second page also fluttered down beside the first one.

"Two pages?" Julie asked.

Emily skimmed the first sheet with Jessie's familiar handwriting. Then she glanced at the second sheet and stared at an unfamiliar scrawl. Intrigued, she glanced at the signature. "Oh!" she whispered in surprise.

"What is it?" Julie asked eagerly, sitting up to face her cousin. "What's it say?"

"I . . . uh . . . haven't read it yet."

"Then do it, and share it with me."

★ ★

Emily hurriedly read the second sheet, and a warm flush tinged her cheeks.

Julie noticed. "Are you blushing?"

"No, of course not!" Emily's sudden denial lacked conviction.

"Oh yes, you are!" Julie jumped down from the high bed and hurried to stand in front of her cousin. "I never saw you do that! Read it aloud, please!"

Disturbed by her own unexpected reaction, Emily protested. "Just a minute. I haven't read the one from Jessie yet."

"Didn't she write both pages?"

When Emily didn't answer, Julie exclaimed, "No, I can see from your face that she didn't! Who's the second one from?"

Emily stalled. "In a minute." She quickly reread the second page, then carefully placed it under the first sheet and skimmed that.

"Well. . . ?" Julie demanded impatiently.

"Jessie says everyone's well, and she wishes I were there."

"What about the second page? Come on, tell me! I can see that you're not telling me everything!"

For another few seconds, Emily hesitated, unsure of what to do.

"Hurry up!" Julie urged. "We can't keep secrets from each other."

"It's not really a secret, I guess," Emily admitted a bit reluctantly. "It's from her big brother, Brice."

"The one you said was always teasing you?"

"He teased both Jessie and me, saying little girls need to be picked on to help them grow up." Smiling at the memory, Emily added somberly, "Now he's joined the army."

"Boys!" Julie exclaimed. "What they won't do to get in a fight, even though they could get killed."

"Don't say that!"

Julie's eyes narrowed suspiciously. "You like this boy?"

It took a moment for Emily to answer. "He doesn't know

★ ★

it, but he's the first boy I ever sort of liked."

"But he's six years older than you!"

"I didn't say we were going to get married! I grew up knowing him and his sister. But . . ." Emily tapped his letter with a forefinger. "He wrote to ask if I would pray for him."

"Pray for him? A Yankee—oh, sorry!" Julie clapped both hands over her mouth in embarrassment.

"It's all right." Emily looked down at the letter. It was an innocent request from a friend's older brother who faced wounding or worse.

Julie dropped both hands from her mouth. "Are you going to do that?"

"Of course. I'll write him back and let him know that I'm praying for him."

"You'd better hurry. Remember what Mama said about no more mail between North and South after May thirty-first."

"I almost forgot." Emily headed for the small desk with its inkstand and pen. "I'll do it right away."

"Don't forget to write Jessie, too," Julie teased.

"I won't." Emily sat down at the desk. "Oh, I wish I could see all my old friends again before this awful war. . . ."

She left her sentence unfinished, chopping off a sudden, frightful image of Brice and other Illinois boys she knew lying dead on some battlefield. At the same instant, she recalled that this very morning Union soldiers had been reported heading toward Briarstone.

A slight shiver passed down her arms as the horrors of what war could do to her and those she knew and cared about washed over her. She shook off the images, fervently thinking, *I wish there were some way I could see Jessie and all my other friends before—* She snatched up the pen to shut out the rest of the thought.

She finished the letter and thought about how to mail it without arousing Uncle Silas's anger. He would not like her writing to a Yankee boy who was becoming a soldier.

★ ★

There was a knock on the bedchamber door. "Miss Julie just left," Emily called, thinking she was talking to one of the slaves.

"This is your uncle. I want to talk to you. May I come in?"

Hurriedly slipping the letter into the writing desk drawer, Emily called, "Of course."

He left the door open but lowered his voice. "I want to talk to you for a couple of reasons," he began. "First, I hope you'll understand why I did not speak to your father the last few years. I considered him a traitor to his native South after he moved to the North and slowly turned against slavery and our way of life."

Emily squirmed in the chair, regretting that the two brothers had become estranged. Her father had twice written Silas in an effort to smooth things over, but Silas had never replied.

He continued. "When I saw you interfere in the auction where that black woman was separated from her children, I realized that you do not understand our ways. You don't know the importance of our labor system. Our whole economy is based on the use of black servants."

"You call them that, but you really think of them as slaves."

Emily saw her uncle's face harden, but he still spoke calmly. "Whatever you choose to call them, we consider them servants. They are important to us. They are given instruction in the Christian religion, and we provide a wagon for them to attend church."

Where they sit in the back behind partitions, Emily thought but kept silent.

"I know some masters are harsh with their servants," Uncle Silas concluded, "but at Briarstone, we care about them. However, we will not tolerate disobedience. I realize that we have a different way of thinking, but after you've lived here awhile, I hope you see our system is right and that you become a real part of our family."

After he left, closing the door behind him, Emily realized

★ ★

that he genuinely meant what he'd said. But she couldn't shake the memory of the black mother and the grief-stricken wails of her children as they were separated forever.

Emily doubted that she would ever forget. Instead, she wondered if that one incident had already begun to change her life forever.

A NEW THREAT

There was a risk in returning to school after William's strong objections, but Gideon desperately wanted to improve his education. The morning after the false rumor about Yankee invaders, Gideon accompanied his younger brother and sister to classes.

The teacher was at the door when the Tugwells approached. William stood behind Mr. Boswell, glaring at Gideon, who stopped at the bottom of the steps with his siblings on either side of him. Nat stood outside by the flagpole.

Mr. Boswell cleared his throat. "Gideon, late yesterday William's father informed me that your brother and sister may continue their lessons, but you cannot."

"But there's only a few more days before classes end for the summer!" Gideon protested.

William quickly stepped up beside the teacher. "They're already over for you, both now and forever!"

Gideon angrily clenched his teeth but didn't reply.

"I'll handle this, William," Boswell said.

"Thanks for letting Ben and Kate back, Mr. Boswell." Gideon gently pushed Ben and Kate toward the door. "And thanks for letting me attend before."

"I'm sorry, Gideon," the teacher replied.

William's smug grin made Gideon want to wipe it off his face, but he knew from experience that he could not do that.

Gideon stole a quick glance at Emily, standing with Julie. Both girls looked sad, but they remained silent.

Walking dejectedly back toward the woods and the shortcut to his home, Gideon fumed in disappointment. His whole future depended on gaining as much knowledge as possible. Now his sole opportunity had been snatched away. Nearing the woods, he kicked at a stone, then turned for a last look back.

Nat was just disappearing around the left front corner of the schoolhouse. *He's got to wait like a dog for his master to come out again*, Gideon thought.

Abruptly, Gideon stopped, frowning. If he returned home, his father would put him to work on some hated job like greasing the wagon wheels or cleaning the barn. Not wanting that, Gideon considered if it was beneath him to talk to the slave boy. Then he remembered the look in Nat's eyes when he was being sold.

Gideon quickened his steps as he again approached the school. The windows were open, allowing the fresh May breezes to enter. Rising on his toes to make as little noise as possible, Gideon rounded the corner where he had last seen the slave boy.

Nat sat with his back to Gideon, his right hand extended to the dirt before him. The teacher's voice could be clearly heard through the open window above him. Still on tiptoes, Gideon approached close enough to see that the slave was writing with his finger in the dirt. Suddenly, he stiffened, hurriedly erasing the marks he had made.

But it was too late. Gideon's eyes opened in surprise. "You can write!" he whispered.

Nat quickly laid a finger over his mouth, then rose to a crouch and scurried away from the school toward the covered well in back. Puzzled, and knowing that it had long been illegal to teach a slave to read or write, Gideon followed.

Behind the small shed that protected the school's water supply, Nat turned to face Gideon. "You going to tell on me?"

★ ★

he asked, his voice holding a hint of both fear and defiance.

Gideon shook his head. "I wouldn't tell your master a thing."

Slowly exhaling, Nat whispered, "Thank you."

"How did you learn to write?"

"I had a kind master, but he died."

"You also read?"

"Yes." There was a hint of suspicion in Nat's tone.

"How well?"

"I suppose I could read any book if I wanted."

A thought flashed into Gideon's mind. "Could you teach me?"

"I rarely am allowed out of William's sight."

Gideon noticed that Nat had not said "my master." "How about when he's asleep?"

"I sleep on a pallet outside his bedchamber near the top of the stairs. But if you're thinking what I think you are, it won't work. If he called me in the middle of the night and I wasn't there, he would whip me very severely."

"Yes, I'm sure he would." Gideon shrugged. "Well, it was just an idea." He started to turn away.

Nat's voice stopped him. "Wait! I've heard William and the young ladies speak of you. You're a farm boy?"

"Yes, why?"

"You ever traveled around Virginia very much?"

"Some. I've gone with my father to Manassas Junction and Richmond a few times."

"Then you know the countryside rather well?"

Gideon sensed an excitement in Nat's questions. "Well enough, I guess. Why?"

Nat's eyes glowed, but quickly they clouded. "Nothing, I guess," he said sadly.

Gideon turned away and headed for the woods, wondering what the slave boy had been thinking but didn't say aloud.

★ ★

★ ★ ★ ★ ★

On the way home after school, Emily made an announcement that startled Julie so much that she stopped dead still in the dirt road.

"You what?" Julie exclaimed so loudly that some of the overseer's children walking ahead turned around.

"Shh!" Emily cautioned, her voice low. "I don't want anyone else to know just yet."

Julie gripped her cousin by both arms. "Why not just send a letter? It's too risky to even think of a trip like that!"

"If I don't go now, I may never again get the chance. Besides, school will soon be out, and I could leave the next day."

"Where would you get the money?"

"I've got a small amount that my parents left me. It's enough to get me there."

"But . . . but . . ." Julie sputtered. "You might stay there, and I couldn't stand that. Having you here is the only thing that gives me hope of hanging on until I'm old enough to marry and move away."

"I know it's hard, Julie, but I'm so homesick and lonely. You've been wonderful, and your parents have been so good to take me in and give me a place to live, but . . . well . . . Jessie's and Brice's letters made me see that I have to go back."

"But it won't be the same! Your family's gone, and Jessie's parents may not have room for you!"

"Mrs. Barlow used to say I was like a second daughter to her. She'll have room, especially with Brice gone to the war."

"No, Emily! You can't! You just can't!"

Emily started walking again, thoughts spilling over each other so rapidly she couldn't seem to think straight. After a few steps she spoke again.

"You heard what Mr. Boswell said today when we reviewed the war situation, starting with the surrender of Fort Sumter, then President Lincoln declaring that an insurrection existed,

★ ★

so he called for a militia of seventy-five thousand."

"After that," Julie took up the review, "on April seventeenth, our Virginia convention voted for secession, but citizens can't vote until May twenty-third. If that happens, Mr. Boswell says Virginia will be invaded, and this state doesn't have the military power to stop it."

"That's why I must go now," Emily said thoughtfully, "while the cars are still running between Richmond and Washington. The nearest place I could catch the train is at Manassas Junction."

"I don't like it!" Julie declared flatly. "And anyway, how would you get from here to Manassas?"

A wry smile touched Emily's lips. "I believe your father and brother would be so happy to see me leave that they would make a carriage available."

"No! No! No!" Julie cried, her voice breaking. "I don't think Papa will hear of it, so please don't try!"

"I must." Emily struggled to keep her own voice steady. "I simply must, so please try to understand."

★ ★ ★ ★ ★

Gideon climbed into the hayloft to pitch the golden stems down to the manger for the mule and the one milk cow. The Tugwells' two hounds flopped onto a forkful of hay that missed the manger and landed on the wooden floor.

Gideon had already concluded that Nat was thinking of running away. That could be the only reason the slave boy had asked how well Gideon knew the Virginia countryside. He wondered if Nat had any idea of how mean Barley Cobb's dogs could be when they caught a runaway slave.

Both of the Tugwell hound dogs suddenly shot to their feet, their long ears flopping about their sad-looking muzzles. Then they barked loudly and raced out of the barn.

Gideon jabbed the fork into the hay and slid down the stack to look out the open door. The Lodges' carriage rattled down the dirt lane toward the small house.

"Oh no!" Gideon moaned aloud. "Why're they coming here?"

Gideon's father stepped out of the harness shed with a horse collar in his hand. "I don't need any trouble with them today," he called to his son as both headed toward the approaching vehicle.

Silas waited for George to stiffly climb down from the high outside seat and open the crested carriage door. William followed him. Neither moved forward to meet the Tugwells but waited for them to approach.

"Afternoon, Tugwell," Silas said with a smile but did not offer to shake hands. "You and the family well?"

"Tolerable enough."

Gideon's gaze shifted to William. He had the same smug smile that had annoyed Gideon that morning. Neither boy spoke while the men went through their small talk prior to getting down to the reason Silas had come.

"How's your oldest boy like soldiering?"

Mr. Tugwell shrugged. "Haven't heard from him since he joined up to fight the Yankees."

"Likely he's over at Camp Pickens."

Gideon's interest shifted back to the planter, who continued. "I hear that's where the Confederate generals are sending thousands of recruits."

"Camp Pickens?" Mr. Tugwell repeated. "I don't recollect hearing that name."

"I'm not surprised. It's a new one right near Manassas Junction."

Old Gideon removed his sweat-stained hat and scratched his head. "I know that place. It's where I take my crops to sell. Railroad runs between Washington and Richmond."

"That's the one," Silas replied. "You might have a hard time getting your produce to market this year."

Gideon involuntarily sucked in his breath. The only real

amount of cash money the Tugwells had all year came from selling the yield of their land to far-off markets that only the cars traveled. What would his family do if they couldn't get their crops to the railroad?

He was relieved to hear his father's stoic answer. "Nobody can force an early crop, and besides, a farmer's life is full of hard times."

The tobacco planter nodded to acknowledge the truth of that statement. He said, "I hear that troops are being shipped in from all over Virginia to defend the rail line in case the Federals attack across the Potomac over the Long Bridge."

"You make it sound like our militia can't stop them from doing that."

"They can't." Silas shifted his gaze to sweep the Tugwell property. "It won't be for the lack of trying, but I know some men in high places, and they say Virginia doesn't have the men or material to stop an invasion."

"They could overrun this whole countryside!" William exclaimed.

Turning to his son, the planter agreed. "They could, especially if they attack on two fronts, like Manassas Junction, and also come up the peninsula toward Richmond."

An image of his geography book spread out in Gideon's mind. Manassas Junction was northeast, with Washington barely twenty-five miles beyond.

The peninsula was southeast, jutting out into the end of Chesapeake Bay. The Potomac, Rappahannock, York, and James Rivers all emptied into the bay. Fort Monroe lay at the peninsula's extreme tip.

Federals could march up the long finger of land plus send gunboats up the James toward Hopewell. Richmond was within easy striking distance from there.

"There's talk that Jefferson Davis and his cabinet are planning to move the capital from Montgomery, Alabama, to Richmond," William announced. "Those blue bellies would like to

★ ★

take Richmond just as we would want to capture Washington."

Silas's eyes flickered back from the rich bottomland with its stand of virgin woods. "I'm a reasonable man, Tugwell. I can survive even if the Yankees come here, but everyone knows you're barely making it now. So I'll make you another offer to buy this place so you and your family can have money to move someplace where it's safe."

"Not for sale." Mr. Tugwell's tone turned cold and blunt. "I told you enough times before, Silas."

Gideon thought he saw the other man grimace at the familiar use of his first name.

"You haven't even heard my offer, Tugwell."

"The answer is still no." Mr. Tugwell picked up the horse collar and turned toward the harness shed. "I got work to do."

Gideon watched him walk away, leaving the planter and his son standing by the coach. Gideon clearly saw the dark flush of anger sweep over Silas.

Wordlessly, he turned and reentered the carriage while George held the door open for him.

William's face was also contorted in fury. He lowered his voice so only the reinsman and Gideon could hear. "You had your chance. If the Federals don't burn you out, then maybe I'll do it myself!"

Spinning on his heel, William almost leaped into the carriage, and George climbed stiffly into the driver's seat. The matched bay team turned the coach around in the yard and headed down the narrow lane toward the public road. Gideon stood watching as instant fear raised gooseflesh on his shoulders and arms.

★ ★

THE INVADERS

With Julie there for moral support, Emily approached her uncle that evening when he came home from a horseback inspection ride around the plantation. Emily was encouraged that he appeared to be in good spirits. She asked if the tobacco crop was doing well.

"Very well," he replied, sitting down in the big entryway so a male servant could remove his boots. "If those Yankees don't invade us, we should harvest a record crop." He paused, glancing suspiciously from Emily to Julie and back again. "What's on your minds?"

"I would like to return to Illinois," Emily said.

"I'm not surprised," her uncle replied. "I heard about the letter from your childhood friend. She probably got you all stirred up, but I can't let you go."

"But Uncle Silas—"

"Please try to understand," he broke in firmly. "You are my brother's only surviving child, so I'm responsible for you. I will provide for your creature comforts until you're grown."

Creature comforts? The words repeated themselves in Emily's mind. She wanted more than that; things like real love and a sense of belonging. It was all she could do to hold back the sharp retort that sprang to her mind, but she yielded to Julie's tug on her arm. They left without a word, although Emily heard her cousin sigh with relief.

★ ★

I'm not giving up, Emily thought while holding back frustrated tears. *Sooner or later, I'll find a way!*

★ ★ ★ ★ ★

The next morning when the school bell rang, by previous arrangement Gideon and Nat cautiously entered the woods by the river. Silently, they stepped out from behind brush and trees to look at each other across a sandy pit ten feet across.

It had been created when high waters gouged away part of the riverbank, partially uncovering large roots of three trees. They remained alive, although leaning a little. Their leaves, along with brush on the bank, hid the pit from casual view.

Gideon almost wished he hadn't come. Two great concerns warred in his mind. If his father found that he had slipped away from his farm chores, even for an hour, he would receive a fierce tongue-lashing. His second concern was because it just didn't seem right for a white boy born and reared in the South to be taught by a slave.

Yet his desperate need to improve his education drove Gideon to take the risk. He slid down the embankment, crawled under the protective cover of the tree roots, and looked up expectantly at Nat.

Nat hesitated, looking down out of troubled brown eyes. If William left the classroom before recess and found his body servant gone, there would be at least a whipping with a broad leather strap that could draw blood at each blow.

Even worse, if William learned that Nat was literate and teaching the hated "poor white trash" farm boy, the slave could be sold down the Mississippi, where his chances for escape to freedom were virtually nonexistent. There was also the possibility that Gideon would betray him.

Nat weighed his dangers against the desire to escape from slavery. Gideon could teach him the geographical landmarks between here and a free state. That knowledge was essential to

★ ★

successfully eluding Barley Cobb and his vicious hounds that would surely be set on his trail.

"I've got to get back before recess," Nat said, easing down into the pit beside Gideon. "What do you want to learn first?"

"I brought a book." Gideon produced *Uncle Tom's Cabin*. "Teach me the meaning of some words I've marked. Then what do you want me to show you?"

Nat had considered how to present his needs without letting Gideon know why they were important. "Rivers," Nat said. "Tell me about the rivers around here."

"Your master must have many books or maps with such places marked. Why don't you use those?"

Nat smiled without humor. "Perhaps you don't know that it is forbidden for us 'servants' to even look at a book." He accented *servants* with a hint of sarcasm.

"You could do it when nobody was watching."

"There are those of my kind on every plantation who would betray one of us for a garment, an extra bite of food, or even a piece of finery, like a pretty ribbon."

Gideon was satisfied that he had correctly guessed Nat's motive in agreeing to meet with him. Like other slaves Gideon had heard about, Nat planned to run away to a free state.

It was necessary to know something of the route, especially rivers and other obstacles that must be crossed. Travel was safest at night, although the aggressive white patrollers were always lurking about. They delighted in catching a runaway without a pass signed by the master or mistress.

The patrollers, called "pattyrollers," were allowed to beat the fugitive before returning him to the master, where more punishment was certain. It was even worse to have dogs catch a runaway because they could inflict horrible wounds before the slave catcher called them off and returned the fugitive to his master for a reward. That was the way it had always been

★ ★

as far as Gideon knew, so he was not disturbed at Nat's unspoken plans.

"My father taught me all the rivers north of here," Gideon explained. "When he was a young man, he traveled with a sutler before turning to farming. So I'll tell you what he taught me."

Hesitating, Gideon mentally phrased a question that would confirm his suspicions about Nat's plans. "While we're at it," Gideon said casually, "maybe you'd like to hear what a farm boy knows about the night sky and how to travel using the North Star as a guide?"

The boys' eyes met and held, and slowly, each let a hint of an understanding smile touch his lips.

★ ★ ★ ★ ★

Late that afternoon, with the sneaked lessons exchanged, Gideon hurriedly finished his chores. He tried to ease his guilt for taking an hour off for a lesson by telling his father that he would cut some trees for fences before supper.

With an ax across his shoulder and both hounds following, Gideon made his way to the river bottom far from the pit school. He neared a stand of young pines just as the hounds bellowed loudly and plunged through the underbrush toward the river.

Hearing girlish shrieks of fright, Gideon yelled, "Rock! Red! No! No, I say! Come here!"

The dogs trotted back, tongues rolling. They fell in beside him as he ran toward where he had heard the cries.

Emily and Julie clutched each other, their eyes wide with fright.

"They won't hurt you," Gideon called.

Julie exclaimed, "I thought they were Barley Cobb's dogs mistaking us for runaway servants."

Gideon tried not to be awkward as he approached the girls. "My hounds only run possum and coon."

★ ★

"Did we trespass on your land?" Emily asked. "The weather is so nice that we went for a little walk."

"It doesn't matter," Gideon replied, lowering his eyes. He swallowed hard, remembering how William had twice humiliated him in front of the girls. Yet he had to express his gratitude to Emily. He forced the words out. "Thanks for sticking up for me the way you did."

Sensing his embarrassment, Emily smiled warmly. "I'm sorry that it happened."

"Twice," Julie said thoughtlessly. "At the slave auction, and then at school—" She broke off at her cousin's quick glance of disapproval.

"Well," Emily said quickly, turning away, "we'd better get back. I'm sorry we wandered onto your land."

"Wait!" The word surprised Gideon, but it just seemed to erupt from him.

The cousins looked expectantly at him while he hurriedly tried to think of what to say. He didn't want Emily to leave, and that thought surprised him, too. "Uh," he began, again lowering his eyes, vainly trying to think of something logical to say. "Uh, what do you think about the war?"

He raised his eyes and looked more confidently at both girls before his gaze settled on Emily.

"We don't get much news," she replied, "but my uncle has friends in the Virginia government, so he keeps us posted on what's going on."

"Such as. . . ?" Gideon prompted.

"Well," Emily began, "he thinks there won't be an actual invasion until after the people of Virginia vote about whether to secede or not."

Gideon frowned. "I thought that was done a few days after Fort Sumter?"

"No," Julie answered. "That's when our Virginia convention voted to secede, but it won't be until May twenty-third that the people vote."

★ ★

"That's next week," Emily interjected.

Her cousin continued. "Right. Papa expects that if we vote to join the Confederacy, Lincoln's troops will promptly invade us and what Papa calls 'our sacred land.' "

"There's no way we can stop them?" Gideon asked, losing some of his shyness. The prospect of having Yankee soldiers around in the next week was scary.

"Not according to my uncle," Emily explained.

"That's true," Julie agreed. "Even though Robert E. Lee has been given command of the Virginia state forces, he doesn't have the men to be wherever the Union might strike. So at Briarstone we're packed and ready to flee if necessary, even though we don't want to leave."

"How about your family?" Emily asked Gideon.

"We're going to stay." His voice was calmer than he felt. He quickly added, "I just wish the Federals would leave us alone."

"They won't," Julie said flatly. "Lincoln is determined to destroy our way of life, and all over slavery!"

"Julie and I disagree about that," Emily explained. "Mr. Lincoln is just trying to keep the Union together."

Julie appealed to Gideon. "What do you think?"

"I never thought much about it. But I know that there have always been slaves, even in the Bible. Some Northern states used to have them, too."

"Even some Virginia churches own slaves," Julie interjected. "Not far from Appomattox Courthouse, one church owns about seventy-five who are hired out for profit. All their earnings go to the church. Once it got seventy-five thousand dollars in one year."

"I heard about that, too," Gideon admitted. "Even though my father's never owned any, I guess it's natural for people to have slaves if they want."

"How can you say that?" Emily cried. "Would you like to be owned like a dog or horse? How would you feel if you were standing on the auction block instead of that mother and her children?"

The girl's voice rose with indignation as she continued without giving Gideon an opportunity to reply. "How would you feel if you were Nat, that boy William now owns? How would you like knowing that from the moment you were born until you die, you are property, not a human being, and without a single right?"

"Easy, Emily," Julie urged. "Gideon has a right to his opinion, and I agree with him."

Gideon stood speechless, surprised at the emotion in Emily's tone. He hadn't wanted to agitate her.

"As I said," Gideon remarked gently, trying to soothe Emily's feelings, "slavery just seems natural, although I never had thought much about it one way or another."

"Then start thinking about it!" Emily challenged.

"Maybe I will."

"Good!" Emily cried triumphantly. "Then we can talk again sometime."

Gideon turned at the sudden bawling of his hounds. "Somebody's coming," he announced, turning with the girls to see two saddled horses a quarter mile away.

"It's my brother and Nat," Julie said in a hoarse whisper. "There's no sense letting him see us. Come on, Emily. Hurry!"

The girls ran into the woods and were quickly lost to sight. Gideon picked up his ax and began chopping at the nearest sapling. Safe on his own land, he glanced back to see William and Nat riding side by side well inside the Lodges' adjoining property.

Gideon was relieved to see that Nat had safely returned to waiting outside the school before William came out for recess with the other students.

Gideon watched William reign in his horse, stand in the stirrups, and sweep the Tugwell land.

"You'll never own this place," Gideon muttered under his

breath, swinging the ax vigorously. "I hate it, but it belongs to us Tugwells, and you're never going to get it."

And you aren't going to burn it down, either. As the sapling toppled over, Gideon added to himself, *Someday, when I'm a writer, I'm going to show him I'm just as good as he is!*

★ ★ ★ ★ ★

It was generally accepted among plantation owners that their servants had an uncanny way of knowing the latest news even before the masters did. So it was the next week when old Uncle George returned from town with the mail and disturbing facts.

At the back door of the manor house, George handed the mail to Nat and whispered the news. "The Union has sent General Benjamin Butler to Fort Monroe. He's up to something; probably going to invade up the peninsula."

There was more, which Nat shared with Gideon when they again secretly met in their pit school the next morning. In the past few days, Tennessee, Arkansas, and North Carolina had all joined the Confederacy. The Provisional Congress of the Confederacy had voted to move the capital from Montgomery, Alabama, to Richmond, Virginia.

"The most important part," Nat concluded, "is that yesterday, May twenty-third, the citizens of Virginia voted three to one in favor of secession."

Gideon sighed heavily, recalling what Emily had said about her uncle expecting Lincoln would not invade Virginia until after the people voted. The Confederate States of America seemed complete with eleven states. Blood was certainly about to be shed in Virginia.

"Does William know this news?" Gideon asked Nat.

"Yes. He'll tell the teacher and the other students, so classes may be dismissed early. I can't teach you today because if William finds me missing—"

★ ★

"Of course," Gideon interrupted. "Go quickly. I'd better get home and tell my family."

Nat reached for a vine to help pull himself out of the pit, then paused to look into Gideon's eyes. "I hope you get whatever it is that makes you want to be literate so much that you're willing to learn from me."

"Thanks. I have already learned a lot. I hope you got what you wanted out of all our sessions."

Nat smiled. "I have enough for my purpose, thanks."

Gideon jogged toward home, but his thoughts leaped back to Emily. Since their last conversation, he had done a lot of thinking about slavery. He hoped to have an opportunity to tell her before the Yankees invaded. After they did, there was no way of knowing whether he would ever again see the girl with the hair as pretty as sunshine on golden ripe wheat.

★ ★ ★ ★ ★

The next morning, Friday, Gideon and his father slipped out of the house before dawn to begin their daily chores. The boy carried a bucket to milk the family's only cow. Old Gideon held the lantern.

The sky was clear and beautiful, Gideon noticed, trying to shake off the knowledge that soon it might be filled with screaming shells and ominous black smoke.

His writer's eye hungrily sought the trees, now freshly adorned in bright new leaves. His mother's lilies of the valley, lilacs, and tulips were ready to greet the coming sun with vibrant colors. The carefully tended rosebushes were thick with buds.

Even the verbena borders valiantly defended their beauty from the dusty yard with its crisscross wagon and hoof marks. Someday he would be able to describe them so others could feel what he did.

"Papa," Gideon asked, "do you think the Yankees will get

★ ★

this far? Could they destroy everything here? Our house? The barn, the smokehouse—"

"If they find us," his father broke in, "they just might."

"Our summer wheat crop," Gideon motioned with his free hand toward the fields. "Can you get it to market before—"

"Can't hurry nature," his father interrupted gruffly. "But it should be ready in mid-July. So when you and your mother go to church this weekend, you'd better all say an extra prayer that I can still get to Manassas Junction and back."

"I'll do that," Gideon said quietly. "And I'm praying every day that Isham will be safe, too."

Wherever his older brother was, Gideon knew he would be one of the few ready to defend Virginia from the invaders. Gideon prayed that Isham wouldn't be one of those killed or wounded.

★ ★ ★ ★ ★

Late the next day, a horseman galloped down the Tugwells' rutted lane from the public road. He shouted excitedly, "Federal troops have crossed the Potomac and taken Alexandria, Fairfax, and Arlington! General Butler's army is also moving up the peninsula between the York and James Rivers, heading for Richmond! This is not a rumor! This time we're invaded for sure!"

ONE WOMAN'S OPINION

All houses of worship in Church Creek were packed that first Sunday after the Yankee invasion. Even Gideon's father, who seldom attended, joined his family at services. There was an awed hush in the plain white frame church with its simple cross on the bell tower.

Prayers were offered for all the young men like Isham Tugwell who had already enlisted, and for those who were flocking to the colors to defend Virginia.

Gideon, stirred by the seriousness of the times, listened as Pastor Caldwell preached an emotional sermon. "Eighty-six years ago," he declared, "our forefathers had valid reasons to take up arms against the king's oppressive government in England. But their grievances were small compared to the tyranny now thrust upon us by Washington."

There were congregational echoes of agreement. "That's so, brother!" one older man said loudly.

Gideon's eyes came back to the preacher, who lowered his voice and leaned across the pulpit. "But we must not give way to hate. We are still to love our enemies, even those who have desecrated our sacred soil. We ask nothing of them except to be left alone, but they want to inflict their will upon us to try destroying our way of life."

Gideon slipped an arm around his little brother. They were poor and looked down upon by Virginia's planter class, but the

★ ★

Tugwells were not slaves. They were not like Nat or the desperate young mother whose children had been sold away at the auction.

It troubled Gideon to think such things. He would like to discuss them with Emily and wondered if she would go walking close to his property again. Gideon decided to make periodic trips there, making it look as if he were chopping down more trees for fences and hoping she might again show up there.

★ ★ ★ ★ ★

The Lodges found their pews in the more formal brick church with its stained-glass windows illuminated by the spring sun. They heard a startling announcement from the visiting bishop. "This will be my last time with you for a while. I am also a captain of artillery, and tomorrow I must report to my battery for service."

A low murmur of surprise swept the congregation. Julie leaned close to whisper in Emily's ear, "I can't imagine a bishop firing a cannon at other people!"

"Even David in the Bible fought wars," Emily whispered back.

"I know, but why couldn't the bishop be a chaplain?"

Emily shrugged. Evidently there were valid reasons why he was to serve one way instead of another. Still, it disturbed her to know that both the Yankees and Confederates worshipped the same Lord who had taught that they were to love one another. Yet now brothers in the same faith would kill or wound each other. *Why?* Emily asked herself. *To preserve the Union, as Mr. Lincoln says, or for the South to save their own way of life?*

A prayer was offered for President Jefferson Davis of the Confederacy, but Lincoln was pointedly omitted. Upset, Emily bowed her head and silently prayed for him. She also asked for God's protection on Brice Barlow, who had asked her to remember him that way.

★ ★

Silently, she wondered how men of the same faith, the same language, and the same culture could call upon the same God and ask for victory over the other. Emily found herself wishing she could discuss it with Gideon.

★   ★   ★   ★   ★

After the Tugwells returned home and changed out of their Sunday clothes, Gideon tried to cheer up his younger brother and two sisters. They did not really understand all that made their elders so quiet and solemn. Gideon fashioned a crosspiece on the end of a stick so Ben could roll a barrel hoop. Kate and Lilly wanted to play fox and geese, so their big brother tramped out a circle in the dusty yard. Ben dropped his hoop to join the game.

The Tugwells' hounds aroused from their usual nap under the high porch and charged down the lane as Barley Cobb approached, riding bareback on a black mule.

Ben whispered, "Wouldn't you know it? He's getting here just in time for another free meal!"

"Howdy," the slave catcher greeted the four youngsters. He slid off the mule and brushed dust from his untidy clothes. "I heard yore pa was needin' another mule to take his crop to market, so I brung Blackie for him to consider."

"Oh sure," Ben whispered so low that only Gideon heard. "Any excuse to eat Mama's Sunday cooking!"

Their father came out the back door trailed by the fragrance of frying chicken. Gideon saw Cobb lick his lips before he smiled at the older man.

"Howdy, neighbor! I was jist tellin' the young'uns about offerin' you my mule for the trip to Manassas."

Gideon's father studied the animal with a practiced eye. Even Gideon could see that Blackie was a mighty poor specimen of a working mule. The way he laid his ears back when Mr. Tugwell approached made the boy sure that the animal was mean. He was a biter and a kicker.

★ ★

"Much obliged, Cobb," Gideon's father said. "We can talk about this later. Won't you join us at the table?"

"Well, now, that's mighty neighborly of you." Cobb tied the mule to a post. "I could use a bite, seein' as how I jist got back from chasin' a couple of runaway—" He paused, glancing at the children. "Runaway black bucks. My dogs done trailed them real good."

"So you got yourself a reward from their owner?" Mr. Tugwell guessed, leading Cobb to the well where a bucket of water and a washbasin rested on an old bench.

"Not this time." Cobb looked doubtfully at the washbasin, strong lye soap, and rough towel. "You know what that there General Ben Butler of the Union army done?"

"Can't even guess," Mr. Tugwell said, using the dipper to pour water from the bucket into the pan. "Help yourself, Cobb. I'll wait. So what did Butler do?"

Gideon shared an understanding grin with Ben and the girls as the trapped visitor reluctantly dipped grimy hands into the basin.

"He refused to give up those runaways that escaped into his lines. Flat out refused, mind you, claiming they're 'contraband of war.' But slaves ain't like guns and things; that's real contraband. Runaways are covered under the Fugitive Slave Act. That says even them Yankee states are obliged to turn all runaways back to their owners. But this general refused and cost me a reward."

Gideon's curiosity suddenly flared into life. "You mean that a slave who escapes into the Union lines down on the peninsula can't be taken back by his owner?"

"So far, that's the sad truth." Cobb ignored the towel to rub wet hands on his dirty pants. "The Union is breaking its own law of the land."

Gideon's eyebrows slid up as an idea leaped full-blown into his mind. Instead of having to travel north to freedom, a fugitive slave could go southeast in the very state of Virginia and be safe.

The underground slave system of knowing all the news before their masters did meant that Nat probably already knew about Butler's actions. Gideon wondered if Nat would try escaping to the closer Union lines on the peninsulas instead of following the North Star to a free state.

★　★　★　★　★

Uncle George had whispered the news to Nat moments before he stood behind William's chair in the great dining room at Briarstone. Behind an impassive face, Nat considered whether to change his planned direction of escape. But he remained alert to his young master's power to crush escape plans, so Nat was ready to hand William the salt or do anything else that would avoid arousing the young master's displeasure.

Other maids and male body servants did likewise with the Lodge family and their guests. The servants were mostly light-colored mulattos. Planters preferred having them instead of darker-skinned people in the great house.

Sunday meals after church always brought together a group of about a dozen visitors to Briarstone. Usually, they were important people from the village, politicians, or owners of neighboring plantations. Today a stout widow named Edna Weems sat directly across from Emily, where she was seated between Julie and William.

"Silas," the woman said, making her multiple chins ripple, "that's enough talk about the war. Did you hear what I said to that Sunday school teacher this morning when she announced she was no longer going to teach the catechism to 'those little black imps'? That's what she called them."

From his place at the head of the table, Uncle Silas said, "No, I missed that, Edna."

"Well, I'm glad I was there to set her straight." Mrs. Weems motioned for the serving girl standing behind her to refill her water goblet.

Mrs. Weems ignored the quiet hostess and again addressed the master. "I reminded her that upwards of four million of the colored race have been brought from heathen Africa and rescued from the foulest of paganism."

Nat's eyes turned to Emily, who suddenly seemed to choke after taking a sip of water from her glass.

"You all right, child?" Mrs. Weems asked her.

"Swallowed wrong, I guess," Emily replied, returning the goblet to her mouth.

Seemingly satisfied, the woman continued, ignoring the slaves who stood silently behind the chairs. "Now, *that*, Silas, is proof that our system of having black servants is ordained of the Lord."

Emily stared at Mrs. Weems in disbelief.

The widow turned sharp black eyes on the girl. "Are you sure you're all right?"

Emily was aware that the five other guests had suddenly fallen silent. There wasn't even the sound of silverware as everyone stared at the Yankee girl.

Aunt Anna, Uncle Silas, and William fastened their eyes on Emily. Julie gave her a discreet poke in the ribs, and Uncle Silas shot her a warning look.

"I'm fine, thanks," Emily managed to say, but the hot blood of dissent scalded through her body.

"Emily, is that your name?" the woman asked, waving a silver fork with the engraved Briarstone crest. When Emily nodded, the matron commented, "I understand you're from the North. Illinois, I believe."

Conscious that her uncle was hurling pointed looks at her, Emily nodded but didn't trust herself to say anything for fear of causing an unpleasant incident.

"I am interested in your opinion, Emily," Mrs. Weems continued. "Perhaps if more Northerners understood our system,

★ ★

we wouldn't have that usurping tyrant in Washington trying to force us to live his way instead of the one we choose. How do you feel about slavery?"

Emily held her tongue while her uncle said smoothly, "Edna, please understand that my niece has only been with us a short time. She lost her family and may prefer to just listen today."

Emily understood clearly what that meant as the tension around the table became so strong that it seemed almost visible.

"Thank you, Uncle Silas." She grasped an opportunity to escape the situation. "May I please be excused?"

"Of course," he replied.

Mrs. Weems laughed, her chins rippling like small waves in a pond. "Silas, I do believe you're trying to keep this Yankee girl from joining our conversation."

Emily pushed her chair back, assisted by the maid assigned to her. "Please pardon me, everyone."

Mrs. Weems raised her voice. "One question first, Emily. Do you believe that it is God's purpose to break up our system of keeping servants?"

Servants? You mean slaves! Emily restrained herself to answer carefully but honestly, "I am sorry to disagree with you, Mrs. Weems, but yes."

"You're excused, Emily!" Uncle Silas said loudly.

She clenched her lips to avoid answering while blood gushed through her body like a fire driven by high winds.

William hissed, "You never learn, do you?"

Without replying, Emily turned away, catching Nat's eyes where he hovered behind his young master. Emily thought she saw sympathy in those dark eyes, but her thoughts were focused on her own internal distress.

As she quickly left the room, she heard the widow saying, "It is impossible for me to believe that it is the Lord's will to destroy this system by a bloody war. I'm amazed that your niece can't see that."

Emily rushed up the wide, curving stairs, her mind ripped by crosscurrents of mental pain. *How am I going to live here and listen to people like her and not speak up? But if I do, I'll wear out my welcome real fast. I've got nobody else to stay with and no way of taking care of myself, especially now that the war's started. Oh, I wish I could go back home to Illinois!*

★　★　★　★　★

The next few weeks were filled with rumors of minor skirmishes between Confederate and Union forces on different fronts in various states. To the Tugwells and Lodges, the critical Virginia clashes were north near Alexandria, southeast on the long peninsula, and another front now opened in the western part of Virginia. There the citizens had strongly opposed secession. There were rumors that this portion of the commonwealth might even break off and join the Union.

Emily, disappointed in being unable to get her uncle's permission to return to Illinois, wrote a letter of explanation to her friend Jessie and a separate one to her older brother. But Emily faced a problem in getting the letters posted before the May 31 deadline when all mail service between North and South would end.

She could comfortably hand Jessie's letter to George, but Emily was a little fearful of giving him the one addressed to Brice. George might say something to the master. Emily did not want to stir up any more trouble with her uncle.

Except for the old coachman, slaves were rarely allowed off of Briarstone, even with a pass. So Emily fretted as the final week before mail stopped seemed to rush upon her.

Then she had an idea and hid both letters on her person while she and Julie began regular evening walks along the river. Their route invariably took them near the Tugwell property line, but usually there was no sign of Gideon.

★　★

★ ★ ★ ★ ★

Gideon was out chopping wood on an evening three days before the deadline when he saw Emily and Julie out walking. They hurried toward him as his hounds bawled and rushed to challenge them. Gideon called the dogs back and grinned in welcome to the cousins.

They first talked of the war and speculated if the fighting would come their way before Emily got around to posing the question she had come to ask.

"Gideon, is it true that your family goes to the village once a week for supplies?"

"We do like most families I know," he answered. "We only buy sugar and other things we can't make or grow ourselves. Why do you ask?"

"I need a favor if you haven't gone yet this week."

"We usually go on Saturdays. . . ."

"Not until Saturday?" she exclaimed. "That's too late! The mails stop running on Friday!"

"I said we usually go on Saturday, but the dogs accidentally knocked over our big can of coal oil. It all spilled, so there's only enough kerosene in the lamps and lantern for tonight. I'll have to get more tomorrow."

Emily's face lit up. "Tomorrow?"

"Yes. You want something from the village?"

"Would you post a couple of letters for me?"

"Sure." Gideon smiled, adding, "I've been wanting to see you so we can talk about what we discussed the last time we met."

"That's great!" Emily extended both letters to him. "Something happened last Sunday that might interest you."

Gideon idly glanced at the addresses on the letters, then frowned and looked again at one. The name Brice Barlow leaped up at him. He felt his face stiffen.

Emily hastily explained, "He's the older brother of my best

★ ★

friend in Illinois. He's just joined the Union army. . . ." Emily left her sentence unfinished as the look reappeared on Gideon's face.

Gideon slipped the letters inside his shirt. "I just remembered something I've got to do at home. Maybe we can talk another time." He picked up his ax, whistled to the hounds, and strode rapidly away, leaving the girls to wonder at his sudden response.

★　★　★　★　★

After Gideon posted Emily's letters, he wondered why it bothered him that she had written to a boy. What did it matter to him to whom Emily chose to write? Yet for days afterward, while he and his father repaired the big wagon for the coming trip to Manassas, the thought of the letter still troubled him.

A FINAL
WARNING

On the last day of school, Emily heard Mr. Boswell announce that he was going to "join our gallant troops." Most eligible men were also enlisting, so it seemed unlikely that classes would resume in the fall.

Silas Lodge called the family together in the library one evening after he returned from another trip to Richmond. Not a single servant was present, which intrigued Emily as she and Julie took their seats with Aunt Anna and William.

Uncle Silas cleared his throat. "The Confederate authorities will soon call to the colors all planters who own less than twenty servants. I have many more than that, but I have decided that it is best to keep the Federals from getting closer. So I have agreed to form a cavalry unit, equipping the men with my own horses, and help stop the invaders before they penetrate deeper into Virginia."

"No, Papa!" Julie exclaimed. "Don't go! What if the Yankees come and you're not here?"

"I don't expect that to happen, but I have already instructed your mother about being ready to flee at a moment's notice if that becomes necessary. Your brother is old enough to assume the role of master, assisted by Toombs, the overseer. In my absence, William will defend Briarstone with Toombs and the servants."

Emily stirred uneasily in her chair while Julie blurted out

★ ★

a question that was constantly on the minds of planters and their families. "What if the servants turn on us? It's happened to others! Or what if they all run away?"

"I have instructed your brother in how to deal with such eventualities." Silas turned to his son and laid a hand on his shoulder. "I'm aware that this is a heavy responsibility, but with God's help, we'll all do our duty until the invaders are vanquished."

★ ★ ★ ★ ★

It was common practice for Confederate men of means to be accompanied to war by a manservant, so Silas Lodge's man, Hermes, prepared to follow his master. Nat was assigned by William to help George load a wagon with some cooking equipment that Hermes would need in camp.

George waited until the quiet, slender Hermes limped into the great house to bring out the master's personal items, including his shaving brush and straight razor.

George asked quietly, "Nat, don't you wish you were going instead of Hermes?"

Nat straightened the trunk in the back of the wagon before answering. "I don't want to be in the fighting."

"Not even if the master is being assigned to duty on the peninsula where the Yankees are trying to advance?"

"How do you know that?"

"From another driver who overheard his master talking. He's going to help keep that Union general, Butler, from reaching Richmond."

When Nat didn't reply, George added, "I also overheard a white man reading from a newspaper. It said that Mr. Lincoln's secretary of war, a man named Cameron, had told Butler at Fort Monroe that he should keep all runaways who come within his lines."

Nat turned to look the older man in the eyes. "Why're you telling me this?"

"Just passing the time is all." George's manner was casual. "This newspaper also said that the general was to put such fugitives to work; even pay them, but not to send them back to their owners. So if it was you going with the master instead of Hermes, you could be close enough to slip through the lines to General Butler."

Nat had always sensed that George knew his intentions, but Nat had also followed the man's advice to trust no one. It was hard to believe that George might be a spy for the master, but Nat didn't want to risk being wrong. Gideon was different because he had guessed Nat's intent, though Nat had never confirmed his escape plans to him.

"Well, I'm not Hermes," Nat said indifferently, turning away. "So why don't you tell him what it said in the paper?"

"Hermes got chewed up real bad one time when he heard about something the white folks call an Underground Railroad. It's not a real railroad at all, just a way some abolitionists have of trying to help people like us escape to the North."

Sighing, George added, "But the dogs tracked him. He's still got a limp from that. He won't risk running again because he would end up with his hide all chopped up like Pete's; maybe worse."

Thinking of the slave with the horribly scarred back brought back vivid memories of what a whipping could do.

Nat started back to the big house where William would expect him, but in that short walk, a new and daring idea began to form in the young slave's mind.

He could write himself a pass. *Please pass the bea* *man Nat, through all lines. He is bringing some* *sonal possessions to camp, where he will* *servant.* It would be signed: *Silas Lodge, C* *Confederate States of America.*

If it worked, Nat expected to soo*
eral Ben Butler's Union camp, a f*
missed shortly after slipping off fror*

dogs were put on his trail? Or what if pattyrollers stopped him before he got that far and suspected his pass was forged?

A shiver passed through Nat's body even though it was a warm early summer day. By the time he had reported back to young William, Nat had made his decision. At the first opportunity, he would be on his way down the peninsula.

★ ★ ★ ★ ★

Gideon and his mother stayed up after the other family members had gone to bed. The boy sat on the bench and leaned over the table by the kerosene lamp. His pencil stub moved across a scrap of paper, while his mother rocked and darned a pair of socks.

"What're you doing?" she asked.

"Trying to write a story." He vigorously scratched out the words and crumpled the paper in his hands. "Why can't I make the words come out the way I want?"

"You'll find them by and by. Just keep trying."

"I feel so much inside of me, but it won't come!" He threw the paper into the woodbox by the cold stove. The late June heat was oppressive because it was not only a warm, humid evening, but every door and window was closed up tight against the night air. His parents felt it was bad to breathe such air because sickness often struck in the darkness.

Gideon slid off the end of the bench and walked to the closed window. He couldn't see anything but still he stood, staring out.

"I've been quietly trying to convince your father that he needs help taking that wheat to Manassas," his mother said. "It's too much for one man in times like these. I told him that Ben, Kate, and I can handle things here for the few days you'll gone."

Gideon's hopes rose. "What did he say?"

"He says he'll take you along."

"Thanks, Mama!"

Smiling fondly, she asked, "Do you look forward to going that much?"

"Sure do." He paused, suddenly not so sure. He did want to get away from the hated farm duties for a while, yet he felt concern, too. Being confined in the heavy wagon for a few days and nights meant he could expect the usual tensions between himself and his stern father. How many times would he find fault with Gideon on that trip? He wished he could enjoy being with him the way he did with his mother.

Gideon slapped at a mosquito flitting around his left ear. "Maybe Isham will still be in camp there," he replied, avoiding a direct answer to his mother's question. "I hope to see him after we sell the crop."

"I'd love to see him, too."

Gideon returned to the table and picked up his pencil. "Maybe he'll tell me stories about the war that I can write when I get home again."

His father called from the lean-to bedroom at the far end of the little house. "You two keep waking me up. Why don't you both get to bed?"

Gideon picked up his pencil, wondering if he and his father ever would get to be close, the way he wanted.

★　★　★　★　★

Emily was surprised one early July afternoon following her uncle's leaving to fight the Yankees. William invited her and Julie to take a carriage ride with him. He didn't offer any e
planation of the reason or destination, but the girls acc

With Nat beside George on the coach's outside sea
sengers rode under a cloudless blue sky past Br
bacco fields, now waist high with a crop near
eral slaves, both men and women, chopp
hoes made in Briarstone's own blacks
the pace set by the fastest black w

The plants had grown so close tog

★　★
113

dirt clods between the rows were not visible to the Lodges. A few field workers, under the direction of the white overseer, stooped low, their backs to the hot sun. They plucked suckers off the broad green leaves so that all the nourishment would be forced into the valuable leaves.

Most of the plants had been topped to force more growth into these leaves. Only a couple of plants had been missed. These were each crowned with a bright yellow blossom. How strange it seemed to Emily that there should be such a peaceful scene when all about her war clouds were about to burst in all their fury.

Emily had no clue as to the coach's destination until the team turned off the public road onto a long, dusty driveway. A small, weathered shack came into view under the trees. Emily sensed trouble when she heard Julie suddenly suck in her breath. She leaned closer to the window to look ahead, then turned to face Emily.

"That's their place!"

Emily didn't have to ask whom her cousin meant. If Gideon was home, it would be the first time she had seen him since he abruptly walked away after accepting her letters to post.

William looked directly at Emily. "I thought you might like to see this."

"See what?" she asked, sensing a purpose she would not like.

"Watch and see how I do what my father hasn't been able to do."

Emily glanced at Julie in alarm.

Julie asked her brother, "Why do you want us along?"

"I thought you, and especially Emily, would like to be present when I show the proper way to deal with poor white trash like old man Tugwell and his uppity son."

Emily said cautiously, "I don't think he's uppity."

"You don't?" William's anger was evident. "It still galls me he dared to force my mother off the road that day, and then he showed up at school bold as you please."

There was nothing Emily could say or do to stop her strong-willed cousin, but she cringed, knowing the pain that Gideon and his family were about to suffer.

George stopped the team and held the door open for the young master. He stepped down, motioning for the girls to stay seated.

Gideon and his father left the big wagon, where they were working, and walked slowly toward William, who was waiting by the coach door.

"I guess you heard by now," William said to Mr. Tugwell, "my father has been made a colonel of cavalry and gone to fight the Yankees."

"So I heard," the man answered softly.

"I see you're getting ready for the trip to market," William said, jerking his chin toward the big wagon.

"In a few more days," Mr. Tugwell replied.

Emily shifted her gaze to Gideon. He glanced down, avoiding her eyes, but she was sure he had been looking at her instead of William.

"I hear there are many troops around Manassas Junction," William commented. "You think there might be some kind of trouble so that maybe you'd lose your crop?"

"He's playing a game," Julie whispered. "Hear it in his voice?"

Emily nodded. She had heard it: casual, neighborly words, yet with a tormenting edge.

"There are worse things than losing a crop, of course," William continued, his tone sympathetic. "Like if the Yankees overran this area—and burned your place and your crops to the ground."

Gideon remembered that the last time William had been here, he had threatened to burn the place. Gideon expected his father to explode in anger as he often did. The boy had known him to literally run men off the place for saying something he didn't like. He was quick with his fists, and faster still with his words, but this time he hesitated while his face flushed angrily.

He took a deep breath and admitted, "That would be worse, sure enough." His voice was still calm.

"Tell you how I might help you out." William spread his legs as though to brace himself. "I'll make you a better offer— I'll buy this whole place for more than my father offered you. One-time offer."

Gideon glanced at his father, expecting him to rush at the impudent visitor and backhand him. Instead, Old Gideon lowered his eyes and seemed to study the ground. "I'll think on it," he said, still with downcast eyes. "Time we get back from our trip, I'll let you know."

Gideon was so startled he exclaimed, "Papa! No!"

His father twisted his head and gave the boy such a withering look that he immediately fell silent.

William visibly relaxed. "How long will you be gone?"

"Better part of a week, if all goes well. Takes two days going and two coming, plus finding a buyer."

"Let's say seven days after you start," William said thoughtfully. "If you're not back by then, I'll figure you changed your mind." He paused, then warned, "I wouldn't like that."

He turned quickly and stepped up into the coach. As William dropped into the seat opposite the girls, Gideon heard him say triumphantly, "I did it! In a little more than a week, this place is mine!"

Gideon waited until the coach reached the public road before he dared say anything more to his father. "You wouldn't really sell our home, would you, Papa?"

For the first time that he could remember, his father's face lost the sternness. He surprised Gideon by reaching out and lightly touching his shoulder.

"Would you have had me grab him by his scruffy neck and toss him into the middle of next week? Think about it, Gideon."

★ ★

Without giving the boy a chance to answer, Mr. Tugwell explained, "If I had done that, what do you think he would have done while your mother and little brother and sisters were here alone?"

A heavy sigh of relief lifted Gideon's spirits, and a slow grin spread across his face. "I have to hand it to you, Papa. You were way ahead of me on this."

A rare smiled touched his father's lips. "I hope you'll remember that sometimes when I do things you don't like. Now, let's finish getting ready for that trip. We've got to beat his time limit!"

He started back toward the wagon with Gideon striding comfortably beside him. Then they both stopped and wordlessly looked in all directions.

Gideon was sure his father and he were thinking the same thing: Would William really wait until they got back? Or would he become suspicious that the older man was stalling? William didn't really need the land. He just wanted the Tugwells off of it because he didn't like their kind.

Gideon had a sudden image of a flaming torch sailing through the air one dark night, then the Tugwell house, barn, and everything else erupting in a crackling fire.

WAR CLOUDS
CLOSE IN

Gideon was half dozing on the wagon seat beside his father when a strange sound jerked him upright. Glancing ahead, he saw gently rolling countryside with scattered stands of woods that hid the source of what he heard.

For two days since leaving Church Creek, the boy had mostly heard the clopping of hooves by their mule team on the dusty road and his father's angry words to them.

Although Gideon was always uncomfortable when in close proximity to his father, the boy was glad that he didn't get a tongue lashing for doing something wrong. They rode in silence, each occupied with private thoughts. The countryside was usually quiet except for the morning and evening call of songbirds.

The exceptions to the rural quiet had been the periodic times when the air was briefly filled with the steady tramp of countless Confederate soldiers or the rumble of their wagons and caissons, which were carts that carried artillery. Some troops wore blue uniforms, while others had gray or butternut. There had been no time to standardize colors.

All seemed in good spirits, confident of victory and a short war, as they sang the popular new war song "Bonnie Blue Flag." A minstrel tune called "Dixie," popular in both the North and South, was also sung, as it had been at Jefferson Davis's inauguration in Montgomery.

★ ★

These encounters had forced the Tugwells' heavy farm wagon off the road with its load of wheat. Father and son tolerated the dust over them as the soldiers passed.

When there had been very long lines of troops, Mr. Tugwell usually had guided the team on detours through less-traveled roads, making them lose valuable time.

The Confederate troops slogging along under the hot July sun were taking the direct route toward Manassas Station. The men were in good spirits, but Gideon was sobered by the number of horse-drawn ambulances bouncing along in the swirling dust.

The sound he had heard was louder now. "You hear that, Papa?" Gideon asked, turning his head to better catch the faint throbbing sound ahead. "Drums, I think. We must be getting close to the camp."

"They're drums, all right." Mr. Tugwell lifted his slouch hat and wiped his perspiring forehead with the back of his free hand. "I hope we can sell this wheat in a hurry and find your brother. I'm anxious to get home."

Gideon wasn't sure if that was because of the possibility of William burning the Tugwell place down, or because of the unexpectedly heavy military activity they had encountered. He didn't ask because he was grateful that his father hadn't found fault with everything he did, as often happened at home. Gideon figured that something heavy weighed on his father's mind.

Some of that anxiety had soaked into Gideon's heart so that he felt an uneasiness he could not explain. He should have been glad to be away from the farm chores. When he took over driving for his father, Gideon found that prodding a mule team over long distances was very aggravating. At times his patience was sorely tried, especially with Blackie, the cantankerous, mean-spirited mule borrowed from the slave catcher.

The only good thing that had come out of the delays was more time to think. Gideon had done a lot of that, especially at night when the mules were hobbled and he and his father slept under the wagon bed. Sleep eluded the boy, so his mind leaped about, popping from concern about the war and Isham, to William and Emily. Gideon regretted abruptly walking off the last time he saw her.

★ ★ ★ ★ ★

"Whoa!" Old Gideon spoke sharply to Napoleon and the borrowed Blackie as they rounded a curve hidden by trees.

A beardless picket with a long bayonet glistening at the end of his musket stepped out from the shade of a roadside tree. He held up one hand as a signal to stop.

The soldier in his new gray uniform approached the wagon. "Where you heading?"

"Manassas Station." Mr. Tugwell motioned to the cargo behind him. "Got some summer wheat to sell."

"You plan to ship it by rail?"

"Sure do, same as every year."

"Not likely this time." The picket rested the musket in the crook of his arm. "All the cars are full of troops. No room for farm stuff."

"What?" Mr. Tugwell asked in disbelief. "If I don't ship this grain, my family and I can't make it through next winter. It's our only cash crop."

"Makes no nevermind to me, mister, but you can't go there. I got my orders."

Gideon offered, "Soldiers are going to need bread, so they need this wheat as much as we need to sell it!"

The picket shrugged. "Maybe you can get a speculator to take it off your hands."

"Oh no!" Mr. Tugwell spoke loudly. "I've seen them in the past. They rob a man blind!"

"Suit yourself, but you can't go down this road." He made a sweeping motion to the right. "Maybe you can circle around and get to Centreville, but the Yankees are sending a whole mess of bluecoats there. Friend of mine seen a Union newspaper saying that."

Gideon caught his breath. "Is there to be a battle?"

"Wouldn't surprise me none if there was." The picket glanced around as though someone might overhear him, although the only other person in sight was another young soldier standing guard fifty yards away.

Lowering his voice to a confidential level, the picket continued. "The paper said that Lincoln has been putting plenty of pressure on his General McDowell to do something fast. Seems like the newspapers and the folks up north are complaining that the president's not getting the war won for them.

"So McDowell got together the biggest bunch of men ever seen in the whole country—something like thirty-five thousand—and they're marching from Washington to Manassas this very day. Aiming to ride the railroad so the bluecoats can ride right into Richmond and take it."

Gideon looked with dismay at his father. "What'll we do? If we get caught in the middle of a big fight—"

His father interrupted, looking down at the picket. "How long will it take that army to get here?"

"Hard to say, but it's so hot they're probably marching slow-like. Probably a few days."

Gideon asked eagerly, "Time enough for us to do what we have to and start home where it's safe?"

"The general don't tell me things like that," the picket replied, "but likely it'll be a couple days yet. Shortest way around to Centreville is thataway."

He swung his free hand to the right, then turned his back on the Tugwells and walked past the team.

Father and son didn't move. Gideon looked expectantly at his father. "What're we going to do?"

"We got to make a mighty hard choice. We'll lose valuable time if we go to Centreville. But if we don't, we can't sell this crop, and nobody will eat at our house this winter. We won't get to see Isham, either."

"We've got to get home before our week is up," Gideon added soberly. "I sure don't trust William."

"I don't, either, but if we go ahead, we could get killed."

As the picket passed close to Blackie, he suddenly laid back his ears and tried to bite.

"Hey!" the soldier yelled, stumbling backward. "You get this ol' mule outta here real quick! I don't want to have to write home and tell my folks that I got wounded by the likes of him!"

"I'm mighty sorry," Mr. Tugwell called, flapping the reins over the team's back. The animals leaned into the harness, and the wagon began to move.

Gideon took a slow, shuddering breath, knowing that his father was right. It was a time for hard choices.

★　★　★　★　★

Dusk settled over Briarstone after a sticky, muggy day. On the second-story balcony overlooking the plantation's tree-lined driveway, Emily watched anxiously as Nat held a coal oil lamp so William could finish reading from yesterday morning's Washington newspaper.

Union mail was no longer delivered to the Confederacy, but the paper had been given to William by a Confederate who had come from Washington on a pass that allowed him to cross the lines.

William read aloud, "'The Federal armies have taken the first step toward taking the new Confederate capital at Richmond by moving toward Manassas.'"

Emily caught her breath. "Manassas?" she repeated.

William lowered the newspaper and looked across at her, then at his mother and sister. "Those Yankees don't want to walk all the way to Richmond, so they're intending to seize the rail line that runs from Manassas right into the capital. But a lot of our troops are at Manassas."

★　★

Emily shifted uneasily in her seat. *Gideon and his father probably are at Manassas by now. If they are still there when the two armies meet . . .*

William declared angrily, "Horace Greeley and his *New York Tribune* have been repeating, 'On to Richmond' for about a month now. But getting there won't be easy."

"Do you think Papa's cavalry will be at Manassas?" Julie asked.

Emily glanced at her aunt, who sat quietly, looking out toward the darkening horizon. She had been in bed two days with one of her frequent bouts of illnesses.

"Cavalry move around a lot." William answered his sister's question with a wide sweep of his right arm. "They're a general's eyes and ears. So yes, Papa could be there to help stop the Yankees."

"What else does that paper say?" Aunt Anna asked.

William noisily jerked the paper up again to read aloud, "'General Irvin McDowell is moving westward from the Potomac in the general direction of Centreville and Manassas with about thirty-five thousand troops.'"

"Thirty-five thousand?" Emily repeated in disbelief.

William again lowered the newspaper. "That's what it says. A few days ago I saw a Yankee paper saying that all their editors had agreed they wouldn't report on troop movements or numbers. Now we see just how much a Union newspaper editor honors his word."

"Did you finish reading it all?" Julie asked.

"There's just a little more: 'The Rebel Congress must not be allowed to meet there on the twentieth of July. By then the National army must hold Richmond.'"

"That's the day after tomorrow," Emily said.

"It's coming up fast," William agreed. He looked across the plantation, now almost entirely engulfed in darkness. "I hope Tugwell gets here before that."

I do, too, Emily thought.

★ ★

"Why?" Julie asked. "I thought you hated them."

William explained, "I certainly don't like them. I just want to finish buying them out so that Papa will see what I can do on my own." He paused, frowning. "I hope old man Tugwell doesn't try keeping me from getting that place."

"I don't think they're that kind of people," Emily said.

"Oh, you don't?" Her cousin whirled to face her. "What makes you a judge of poor whites?"

Emily hadn't meant to start defending Gideon or his family, but again her candor had tripped her up. She hesitated before saying, "They just don't seem like it."

"And I'm sure you don't know what you're talking about!" William glared at her. "I wouldn't put it past that old man to try stopping me from what I set out to do."

Julie gave Emily a warning look, so she didn't say anything more and let the matter drop.

William scowled. "If they're late getting back because they're trying to find some way to keep from selling out to me . . ."

He let the sentence hang, causing Emily to look at him in alarm. "What?" she prompted.

A slow smile touched William's lips. "I just wouldn't wait for them to get back," he said smugly.

Alarmed, Emily asked, "What do you mean?"

"Never mind," he said and walked back into the house, trailed by his body servant.

Emily noticed that Nat seemed to have a spring in his step, which puzzled her. His face, as always, gave no hint of what he was thinking. Still, Emily sensed something in his manner that contrasted with concerns her family had discussed.

She knew that he had to go wherever his young master commanded, just as a dog or horse must obey. Yet there was something about Nat that intrigued her because he was unlike other slaves on the plantation. She wondered what was going on in his mind.

★ ★

★ ★ ★ ★ ★

Nat's thoughts made it difficult to sleep that night. He lay on his pallet in the hallway outside of William's room. Nat could hear the steady breathing of personal maids from their makeshift bedding at the top of the stairwell or the first landing.

It seemed certain that the first major battle of the war was about to begin. No matter which side won, there would be a great upheaval, with troops either going toward the fight or running from it. If either victorious or scattered remnants of defeated military units came to Church Creek, it would create confusion in which Nat would risk his life to escape.

Yet even if he eluded Barley Cobb and his vicious bloodhounds and safely reached Union lines, Nat's mission was not done. He had to somehow return to the seemingly impossible task of finding and rescuing his mother, three brothers, and one sister from their slave masters.

Nat's mind leaped and plunged, rising from heights of memories of the days when his family was intact to what had happened since his first master died.

Nat never knew his father but lived with his mother and three younger brothers and a sister, who all had different fathers chosen by the master. Still, the master had been a kindly man who was killed when thrown from his carriage. His heirs had sold the slave family to a trader on the promise that they would not be separated at resale.

Once the trader had possession, he privately sold Nat's mother and siblings to individual buyers. Only Nat, nearing prime age for a young male slave, was held for auction, since he was expected to bring a higher price.

In the cold, smelly slaveholding pens, Nat had cried himself to sleep that first night alone. He had heard from other slaves that once a family was separated, they probably would never again see each other.

★ ★

There had been no rest in sleep, for Nat had dreamed about his family. Unknown to anyone except Nat, his mother had not wanted a white father for her first born but had no choice. In her grief and bitterness, she had named the baby after Nat Turner. He was a slave leader who was hanged in 1831 following an abortive uprising against white masters. Nat's mother had often whispered to him the story she had heard about Turner. The leader had fled into a swamp after the rebellion failed but was eventually caught and hanged.

Nat's mother admired the rebel black leader's spirit even though white folks hated him, fearing other slave revolts.

It was a person's belief and desire, his mother had said, that gave them strength to go on in spite of impossible odds. She longed to be free, but her greater love was for her children, who were eventually sold.

Sometime in the darkness of the slave pens, amidst the filth and the hopelessness filling the foul air with fear so strong that he could smell it, Nat recalled his mother's exact words.

"It's the mind, not the muscle, that counts." Her voice was soft and melodic, soothing as a mother's lullaby in his memory. *"The Bible says, 'As a man thinks, so is he,' and 'let it be as you believe.' Don't forget that, Nat."*

That was the last time Nat cried, for he awoke the next morning determined that he would not weep again. He had first comforted himself with the thought of seeking revenge on the treacherous, lying trader. Nat had not done that, although at the auction he had almost lost control. His mind had triumphed, replacing his original idea of revenge with another.

He would find his way to freedom, then somehow find his mother and siblings and lead them to freedom. He could use his mind and his ability to read and write to do the impossible.

Soon, he told himself as he finally drifted off to sleep outside of William's bedchamber, *the armies will fight near Manassas. When all whites concentrate on that, I'll start toward freedom and find my family again.*

★ ★

CAN'T OUTRUN A
MUSKET BALL

Gideon awoke under the wagon before dawn Saturday morning. He was aware of an ominous stillness. For a moment he lay motionless, staring up at the bottom of the wagon bed, now empty of its grain cargo. His father had been forced to sell it at a loss the afternoon before. A speculator had convinced Mr. Tugwell that it was better to take what they could get and escape with their lives.

Gideon tried to understand the quietness. Usually the morning air was filled with the clear, sweet call of cardinals or other Virginia songbirds, offset by the raucous cries of crows. But today, July 21, 1861, there was only a scary silence.

Then a booming drum suddenly broke the quiet, followed by the indescribable sound of thousands and thousands of men stirring from their military tents.

Gideon's eyes snapped to the invisible compartment built into the underside of the wagon bed. The gold coins, carefully wrapped to prevent any telltale clinking, were hidden there. Satisfied that it was still safe, the boy gripped the old family musket that had been brought along to guard the cash.

He crawled out from under the wagon to glimpse a vast, swirling mass of men. He searched his aspiring writer's mind for words to describe it, but the best he could come up with was the image of a headless monster. It rippled like a crawling caterpillar, except this monster was so long it seemed to have no beginning or ending. Yet it stirred with a steady purpose.

Behind him, his father spoke in a voice still thick with sleep. "Something's up. Harness the team and let's get out of here while the getting's good. I'll go see if I can find out which is the safest way home."

Gideon needed no second prodding. He leaned the musket against the wagon bed, picked up the creaking leather harness, and approached the hobbled mules. Blackie laid his ears back and showed wicked teeth.

The boy spoke sharply. "Mind your manners, old mule, or I'll make you wish you had." With his left hand, he lifted the bit toward Blackie's threatening mouth. With his right, Gideon held the harness ready to deliver a sharp blow.

The mule's lips closed and the ears raised. "That's better," Gideon said approvingly, easing the bit into place. "I figure you don't want to get killed any more than we do."

He had both Blackie and Napoleon backed into place beside the wagon tongue in record time. The long ears of both animals twitched nervously, swiveling to catch the rising volume of men preparing for battle.

Gideon's heart seemed to thump in time with the increased beat of the military drum while he eased the lines back over the mules' backs. He looped the lines loosely around the wooden brake handle beside the high wagon seat. He was greatly disappointed that it had been impossible to see Isham due to urgent preparations by troops at Camp Pickens. Gideon wanted to see how his half brother liked military life and to tell him that he had decided to begin a journal.

Gideon's gaze skimmed the small community of Manassas Junction in the distance. He and his father had not been allowed to approach the railroad and two small wood-burning locomotives. They had puffed in on the single-line track from the Shenandoah Valley yesterday to disgorge what seemed like thousands of Confederate men.

The grain speculator had said these might be from General

Joseph E. Johnson's command, or maybe more of Thomas T. Jackson's small force. All had been rushed to reinforce Beauregard's threatened Confederates. It was rumored that somewhere around twenty-two thousand Confederate troops were on hand or coming to meet the Union's thirty-five thousand. A total of more than seventy-seven thousand soldiers were obviously preparing for the first major engagement of the ninety-day-old war.

"Papa?" Gideon called aloud, trying to catch sight of him in the shifting mass of people. The boy's eyes lifted, scanning the horizon. Nearby, Bull Run Creek meandered along while the low Bull Run Mountains raised humps against the skyline. Closer to Manassas Junction, the rolling countryside was level enough for a battlefield. Gideon's eyes moved on, attracted by another locomotive trailing smoke and cinders as it slowed to approach the junction.

That train was literally covered with men. They sat on the roof or waved from freight cars with open sliding doors. For the first time in history, railroads were being used for the rapid deployment of troops from one area to another. The soldiers cheered at the sight of women in hoopskirts waiting with baskets of refreshments. Some were as young as the Confederates' sisters, but many were old enough to be their mothers.

They're going to fight the Yankees, Gideon mused with a lump trying to form in his throat. *Some are going to get killed. So will Papa and I if we don't get out of here. Where is he?*

Anxiously, Gideon looked at the single railroad track stretching south toward the new Confederate capital at Richmond. Yesterday, the grain speculator had said, there had been nearby small but sharp skirmishes between Federals on scouting missions and Confederates digging in along an eight-mile line.

But a body couldn't trust rumors, the speculator had warned, sighing as he counted out the twenty-dollar double-eagle gold coins Mr. Tugwell had insisted upon receiving for his wheat.

Today, the speculator had added, the Congress was going to meet in spite of what the Northern newspapers had said. President Davis wouldn't be there, but his speech would be read to the members. Davis, a West Point graduate, was rumored to be heading for Manassas to offer his support and advice to the Southern commanders.

"Gideon!" His father's voice spun the boy around. "Get seated and untie those reins!"

It had been a long time since Gideon had seen his father running, and even longer since he saw fear show in his face. The sight was enough to make the boy snatch up the musket, clamber over the wooden front wheel, and loosen the lines from the brake lever.

"Gimme those!" his father exclaimed, leaping into the wooden seat beside Gideon and seizing the reins from his hands. "Grab on to something," his father added tersely, clucking to the mules and snapping the lines over their backs. "The whole world's about to blow up around here!"

Clutching the side of the wagon seat with one hand and the gun in the other, Gideon felt his heart increase its tempo to where it seemed about to burst through his ribs. The mules were forced into a reluctant trot, and the empty wagon swayed dangerously as Mr. Tugwell made a half circle, then rumbled away from town.

The dust rose in twin rooster's tails behind them, while the sound of the drum faded. Off in the distance, a cannon boomed, then another, still closer.

"Is it starting, Papa?" he asked anxiously, but his father was concentrating so hard on driving that he did not reply. A shell screamed overhead, making Gideon instinctively duck down. He wondered if they would ever see Isham again, if he and his father would make it safely home, and if he would live to become a writer.

★ ★

★ ★ ★ ★ ★

Emily heard steps on the upstairs hallway and hurriedly slid a sheet of paper into the top drawer of the writing desk. She replaced the pen in the holder but was still seated as the door opened. She breathed a sigh of relief as Julie entered.

"Who did you think would enter here without knocking?" Julie approached and looked down into her cousin's face. "What were you doing?"

Emily wasn't sure why she felt some embarrassment, but she did. "I'm starting a diary, but I don't want anyone to know."

"A diary? What for?"

"Lots of reasons." Emily stood and straightened her skirt. "I get frustrated in not being able to say all that's on my mind, so this gives me a way to get my thoughts down on paper. Someday, when we're both grown and married, maybe our children will want to know what it was like during the war. So I'm sort of writing for them, too."

"Don't let my brother find anything you write that sounds like Yankee thinking."

"I plan to keep it hidden." Emily slowly surveyed the room. "Where would be a good place?"

"I don't know." Julie leaped up to land on the high four-poster bed, her feet dangling well off the floor. "Do you think about who you might marry someday?"

"Not really." Emily inspected the tall armoire against the far wall but found no hiding place for her new diary. "Do you?"

"Lots of times, only there's nobody around here I would want to marry. Still, I've got to get out of here in the next couple of years or so, or I'll lose my mind. That brother of mine—"

She interrupted herself to ask, "Do you know what I heard him saying to his new body servant a minute ago?" When Emily shook her head, Julie explained, "He said to be sure his fastest horse was saddled about sundown. Said he was tired of waiting for old man Tugwell to get back, and so he was going to throw

★ ★

a scare into his wife and little kids."

Emily whirled around to face the other girl. "What kind of a scare?"

"I don't know. But he's so determined to show Papa that he can run those Tugwells off that he might try again. Sometimes I don't know how he could be my brother, we think so differently."

A silent alarm throbbed a warning in Emily's head. "You don't think he actually would burn them out as he threatened?"

"I wouldn't put it past him. Say, how about your friend's brother in Illinois—would you marry him?"

Emily didn't reply. Her thoughts focused on what William might be planning against Mrs. Tugwell.

Julie's voice became dreamy. "He's only six years older than you. That's not very much by the time you're both grown. He must think a lot about you to write—most eighteen-year-old boys don't notice girls our age. Is he handsome?"

Emily still didn't reply but walked to the window and looked out over the plantation. Everything seemed so peaceful and quiet. But what would it be like tonight at the Tugwells'? Should she try to do something to stop William from whatever he planned? If Gideon and his father were there, she wouldn't be so concerned.

She exclaimed aloud, "I hope they get home before tonight!"

★ ★ ★ ★ ★

Gideon and his father had only gone a few miles when they ran into a delay. Two sentries blocked their way with glittering bayonets on musket ends.

"Now what?" Gideon whispered as the taller soldier approached.

"Can't go no farther this way," he declared firmly, looking up at the Tugwells on their wagon seat. "This is a restricted area. Could be shooting here any minute."

"But we've got to go this way," Mr. Gideon replied. "We're running out of time, and our family's home alone."

"Mine, too, mister. A wife and a new baby boy, plus my folks. But I got to keep Yankees from getting to them. We aim to stop them here. I'm powerful sorry, but you can't go this way."

"There is no other way!" Mr. Tugwell protested. "We just came from Manassas, and we know that for a fact."

"Like I said, mister, I'm sorry, but I can't let you pass this point. You've got to turn back."

For a moment the desperate look on his father's face made Gideon think he was going to whip up the team and try to break through. But mules couldn't outrun a musket ball.

"When I was working with that sutler," his father told Gideon, "once we went from Centreville up into the Shenandoah Valley and came back down the west side, then across to our place. It's out of our way, but if we move night and day, we might still beat William's time limit."

"The Federals are at Centreville," the sentry broke in, sending Gideon's heart sinking. "General McDowell is supposed to be getting ready to attack our troops on the other side of Bull Run Creek any time now."

Gideon looked hopefully to his father, knowing that he was thinking the same thing: those left at home were sure to already be sick with worry. Further delay could make them frantic.

Mr. Tugwell took a long, slow breath and blew it out. "It's our only chance, and with the wagon being empty, we can make better time than we did coming."

"You mean go right into Centreville, Papa? With all the Union soldiers there?"

"They probably won't pay any attention to a couple of poor dirt farmers like us. They're all going to be so busy getting ready to fight that they may not even notice us if we drive straight through."

★ ★

Gideon thought about the hidden gold but was afraid to say anything in case the sentries might overhear. "I guess we better do whatever you think best, Papa."

"Ride right into the enemy's center and on to the Shenandoah," his father mused. "Mighty, mighty risky."

Shenandoah was an Indian word meaning 'Daughter of the Stars.' Gideon's love of words stirred at that, but his blood froze in his veins at the dangers that lay in that direction. But was there less danger anywhere?

"Well, mister?" the sentry said impatiently. "I can't let you block the road no longer."

"I understand. We're leaving." Mr. Tugwell clucked to the team and began turning them around. "Gideon," he said softly, "the good Lord probably wouldn't recognize me if I tried to speak to Him after all this time, but I'd be obliged if you said a little prayer."

Gideon bowed his head, feeling very unworthy, but it wasn't just for his father and him that he asked. It was for his mother, brother, and sisters.

Minutes later, father and son groaned when the wagon broke an axle. A new one had to be hurriedly made from a freshly felled tree, but more precious time slipped away.

At sundown, they reached Centreville, now filled with thousands of blue-coated Union troops. They were so thick that Gideon could have almost stepped on one. Fortunately, they had more important matters to attend to than question a farmer and his half-grown son.

It was to be a moonlit night, but traveling then could make the Yankees suspicious. The Tugwells were forced to camp in a grove of trees just outside of town. They could hear and see troops moving out of Centreville toward the Confederate lines at Bull Run Creek.

Gideon tried not to shiver with the fear that ravaged his mind and body. With no other alternative, he and his father finally yielded to tension and weariness. They slept fitfully

★ ★

under the wagon until about five-fifteen in the morning. That's when a whole battery of Union artillery began firing in unison.

Gideon jerked upright, smacking his head against the wagon's underside.

His father was already awake. "I think we're too late," he exclaimed. "The main shooting's started, and we're right smack dab in the middle of it! We've got to run for our lives!"

★ ★ ★ ★ ★

Emily awoke with a start that Sunday morning. She sat up in the high bed, her heart pounding. What had awakened her? Distant thunder? She started to lie back down but stopped. It didn't sound quite like thunder.

Throwing back the covering sheet, she slid down to the hardwood floor and padded barefooted to the window. There wasn't a cloud in the early morning sky, yet the muted booming continued from the north. She searched the horizon for signs of thunderheads, but there were none. Then she whispered, "I think that's cannon fire!"

She started for the next bedchamber to awaken Julie but halted to take another look out the window. For a moment she stared, mentally locating the area near the swamp by the Tugwells' farm.

She counted how many days Gideon and his father had been gone, and a terrible fear gripped her. *They're about out of time, but if that's cannon firing and they're caught in it, William may not wait!*

DAUGHTER OF
THE STARS

Gideon ran to the mules while the rattle of musket fire joined the booming of cannons. The borrowed mule reacted to the boy's rush by turning suddenly and kicking hard with a hind leg. Gideon jerked his head aside so that he heard the whistle of the hoof past his ear.

"You dumb mule!" he yelled, his voice high with fright. "Hold still, or you'll get us all killed!"

Blackie swiveled his ears back, swung his long head around, and snapped viciously at the boy's arm. The long brown teeth closed on the harness where it lay across human flesh. Gideon dropped the leather and looked fearfully at his arm. It was untouched.

Mr. Tugwell rushed upon the stubborn animal, holding the musket by the barrel. Instantly, Blackie repented of his behavior, raised his ears, and stood quietly. The man lowered the weapon to the ground and snatched up the harness where his son had dropped it.

"Get Napoleon ready," Mr. Tugwell yelled. "I'll handle this one!"

Looking across Napoleon's broad back while the harness was quickly worked into place, Gideon saw gray and black smoke rising from the Union batteries in the distance. *Hurry! Hurry!* he told himself, forcing his eyes back to the task at hand.

★ ★

In record time both animals were standing patiently on either side of the wagon tongue while battle smoke started drifting across the brightening horizon.

"Climb in, Gideon!" his father shouted to be heard above the rolling thunder of heavy artillery.

It was an unnecessary command. Nimble and quick as a squirrel, the boy scrambled over the front wheel and plopped down on the seat beside his father.

Old Gideon yelled to the mules, slapped the reins sharply across their backs, and the empty wagon lurched out of the sheltering trees and into a trot.

Gideon couldn't believe the scene spread out before him. Centreville was alive with Union troops being marched double-time toward the sound of battle. The air rang with shouted orders, the jangle of officers' swords, the fearsome clang of bayonets being fixed to muskets, and drums beating like faint echoes of the cannons' deep voices of doom.

"How far to the Shenandoah?" Gideon cried, trying to be heard above the din.

Before his father could reply, the right front wagon wheel hit a tree stump. Gideon was aware of being thrown violently through the air as the wagon tipped over. The mules screamed almost like humans as they fell hard in their tangled harnesses.

Gideon saw the hard earth rushing toward his face. He threw out both hands in an effort to break his fall, but his arms collapsed and he landed headfirst. There was an explosion of tiny white lights in his head, and then he slid wildly down a long, dark tunnel that suddenly ended in total silence and blackness.

★　★　★　★　★

Nat had been sent by his young master to tell George to bring the carriage around. In the stable, with the clean smell of hay and the cheerful morning sound of roosters crowing, Nat silently watched the old reinsman harness the team.

"Something on your mind?" George asked.

After a moment's reflection, Nat decided that he had to take a chance to try gaining the information he needed.

"Uncle George," he began respectfully, "since you're the only one of us allowed off the plantation on any kind of regular basis, you must see a lot out there."

A knowing grin tugged at the old slave's mouth. "You mean on the public roads?"

"That, and wherever else you drive for William." Nat was the only slave at Briarstone who privately referred to the planter's son in such a familiar way. To everyone else, he was always the master or young Master William.

"I see many things," George replied, giving the nearest horse a pat to indicate the harnessing was done. "Why, I have even seen pattyrollers lurking around just waiting to catch some black person trying to run away."

Nat caught a glint of humor in the man's eyes and knew he was playing a game. As discreet as Nat had been, Uncle George had discerned his real interest.

"You have?" Nat replied, trying to draw out more information without saying anything that could get either of them in trouble if questioned.

"Many times." George ran the reins back over the teams' backs and tied them to the metal rail in front of the high seat. "They don't keep a regular schedule but just sort of drift around, mostly at night, of course. That's when most slaves try to escape, their eyes on the North Star. It helps guide them toward free states.

"With most of the able-bodied white men gone off to fight the Yankees," George went on, "only older men are still around to do the patrolling. But most white folks are scared of us black people rebelling against those who are left, so I heard some pattyrollers aren't as mean right now. They don't want their womenfolk murdered."

That news encouraged Nat. "You ever hear of anyone

slipping safely past the patrollers?" he asked.

"Yes, a few. Even now those who get caught find out real quick that some of the older white men can still be mighty mean to a runaway when caught. Of course, people around here are most afraid of Barley Cobb and his dogs."

Nat nodded, remembering Pete, the slave with the network of scars on his back, and Sarah, the girl with the iron shackle on her ankle.

Depending on his temperament and the example a master wanted to make on his other slaves, a runaway could be whipped so severely that he or she could be permanently scarred as Pete was. Nat believed William would be worse than his father when it came to punishing a slave who tried to escape.

George climbed stiffly into the driver's seat. "I see you're thinking real hard." He motioned for Nat to climb up beside him before adding, "The only problem the dogs have is when a runaway gets into the swamp. Hounds can't trail much in there, but most people can't survive in there, either. Some, including runaways, have gone in and never come out."

Nat thought about how Nat Turner had hidden in a swamp after his uprising against white owners failed thirty or so years before. But somehow, the man for whom Nat was named had been captured and hanged along with some of his fellow insurrectionists. Nat figured a swamp was for hiding, but he wanted to go down the peninsula.

The team pulled out of the barn and headed toward the big house. The distant thunder of heavy artillery continued before George spoke again.

"When that big battle is over," he said, his voice low, "this plantation could be overrun with soldiers either running in defeat or marching in triumph. There could be more confusion than you'll ever see in your whole life."

Nat looked questioningly at the old slave, but George kept his eyes on the path leading to the big house.

★ ★

George continued. "There might be so many that the pattyrollers won't be out looking for runaways. There might even be so many tracks of soldiers and horses that no hound could follow a single person's trail."

"Yes," Nat agreed, his mind made up, "I suppose that could happen."

★　★　★　★　★

Emily's concern about what William might do to the Tugwell place if they didn't get back on time tempted her to face William directly. However, she tried to restrain herself and take an indirect approach. She came down to breakfast to find him alone. Even his ever-present body servant was absent.

"You're up early, William," Emily greeted him. "The sound of cannon must have awakened you, as it did me."

William wiped his mouth with the napkin. "I heard it. Probably means a big battle going on. I hope Papa doesn't get hurt if he's involved."

"I pray he's safe." She added silently, *Gideon and his father, too*. Emily fished for words to draw William out. She asked, "Do you suppose the Tugwells could have gotten caught in the battle and may be late returning?"

"We had a deal, so excuses don't count. They're about out of time." He stood at the sound of a team stopping outside. "Well, I have to go somewhere."

He walked out quickly, leaving Emily frustrated and with no answer to the question that troubled her. Maybe she and Julie could take a walk along the river bottom. She would feel better if she could see if the Tugwells' home was still safe.

★　★　★　★　★

Slowly, ever so slowly, the blackness slid silently away, and Gideon sensed light ahead. He lay still, trying to understand where he was. Then he realized his eyes were closed, but

★　★

sunlight was beating against them and a giant drum thumped inside his head.

Very slowly, he opened his eyes and found himself looking into a big black face with a scraggly beard and deep brown eyes. The face split into a grin and turned away. A kind of grunt came from the mouth, but no words.

Instantly, Gideon's father leaned close. "Can you hear me?" he asked.

Gideon tried to answer, but the effort hurt his head. He forced a slight nod.

"Thank the Lord!" Tears sprang to the father's eyes, and he bent quickly to hug Gideon.

As his father let go and stepped back with a loud sniff, Gideon tried to sit up, but the pounding drum in his head grew louder, and black wisps of something seemed to fill his eyes. He lay back again. That's when he realized his head hurt something fierce and there was a big bandage on his forehead.

"Don't try to move just yet," his father cautioned. "Rest a little longer."

A point of fear penetrated Gideon's mind. To avoid the panic that threatened to seize him, he glanced around. Beyond the big stranger in his rough slave's clothes, the boy saw the wagon with two wheels in the air. Napoleon stood trembling nearby, his side bloody and his head hanging. He had been cut free from the harness. Blackie was crumpled across the wooden wagon tongue, which was splintered and covered with blood. Gideon knew without being told that the mule was dead.

"What . . . what happened?" Gideon asked, bringing his eyes back to his father's tired face.

"Tell you later. Right now you just rest, son."

It was the first time he ever remembered his father calling him that. The thought snapped back like a turtle's head withdrawing into the shell. "The gol—" he started to say, but his father's rough hand came down firmly on his mouth, stopping the word.

★ ★

"Everything's safe." His father's voice was so low that the words were barely audible to the boy.

"This man," Mr. Tugwell went on more loudly, "was the only one who would help me. Everyone else was either afraid to come outdoors, or else they headed toward the battle. He tried to get a doctor for me, but they were all busy with wounded men. So he brought some cloth for a bandage and helped patch you up."

Gideon forced a question out of the fear that still held him. "How . . . how bad am I hurt?"

"You got a mighty mean knock on the head, and you were out cold for hours. But the bleeding's stopped and you should be up and around shortly."

Gideon glanced at the sky. The sun had passed its zenith. "It's afternoon already! William! We're going to be too late. . . ."

"Easy! Easy!" His father gently pushed the boy's shoulders down as he tried to sit up.

Mr. Tugwell turned away to watch the black man walking back toward the woods, away from town. "I'm mighty obliged," he called after him.

The stranger didn't answer but kept going.

"I think I can sit up now," Gideon said. He shoved down with his hands. They smarted from where they had been scratched and cut in the fall. Slowly, with his father's assistance, Gideon sat upright. He had only a slight sense of dizziness, which quickly passed.

"What do you think?" his father asked. "Can you make it to your feet?"

"I think so. We've got to get home fast!"

Supported by his father, Gideon stood. His knees felt a little wobbly, but they held him. Smiling in relief, he turned to look around.

The whole war scene again burst upon his vision. The Union troops were gone from Centreville, replaced by a few men in civilian clothes and boisterous women in hoopskirts and decorated hats. They carried picnic baskets and parasols away from the railroad and carriages toward the sound of battle.

Bewildered, Gideon followed them with his eyes, hearing their laughter and loud talk, punctuated by the pop of a cork exploding from a champagne bottle.

"Most of them got off the train from Washington a while ago," Old Gideon explained. "Some came in carriages. I could hear them talking loud enough to wake the dead. They're planning on watching the battle and then riding the cars straight into Richmond. There are a few Union men, too. I heard one of them called 'Senator' and another 'Congressman.'"

"The Yankees whipped us?" Gideon asked in alarm.

"Fight's been going on for hours, but it's not over yet." Mr. Tugwell gently laid a hand on his son's arm. The incredible sight of women heading toward the battlefield with picnic baskets was more than the boy's imagination could grasp. "They could all get killed!"

"Reckon they could. Lead from muskets and exploding shells from big guns don't always pick their targets."

A part of Gideon's brain had not seemed to function, but suddenly it slid into place when he saw the sky now dark with smoke, and his nostrils filled with the acrid odor of burned gunpowder. The cannons still roared in the distance and small-arms fire sounded. These were louder now, and closer. Much closer.

Gideon could hear faint yells; yells of anger and hope and faith. Rebel yells. He was sure of that, although he had no idea why. Then he realized why he was sure. They were men defending their homeland from an invader. Cries of courage.

The first sign of the tide turning against the Union was a pair of cavalry horses without riders running blindly back the way they had come. Right behind them, some artillery horses, free of their guns, charged into sight with traces flying. These were followed by three Union cavalry mounts, running awk-wardly, heads turned in an effort to avoid stepping on their trailing reins.

Gideon remembered the race he and his father had begun toward the Shenandoah Valley. He whirled about. "Papa! We have to get home before William—"

The words died on his tongue. His eyes landed on the dead mule borrowed from the slave catcher, and bloody Napoleon still standing with head hanging.

Now aware of their desperate situation, Gideon turned to his father. "Can that black man help us?"

"I don't think so. He's gone just like he came. A few hours ago he showed up out of nowhere and helped me with you. Never said a word. Just made sounds, so maybe he can't talk. If it hadn't been for him—"

Mr. Tugwell's voice broke, and he spun away so Gideon couldn't see his face.

Slowly, against his will, Gideon let himself face the truth. They were in the middle of thousands of Union troops, with no way home. "Papa, I feel fine now. We can start walking. . . ."

"Look!" his father shouted.

Gideon followed his father's pointing arm. A Yankee soldier ran away from the sound of battle, throwing off his pack and dropping his gun to run unencumbered. To his right, two other Federal infantrymen dropped their canteens and knapsacks. Another even cast off his hat.

They dodged a runaway team of six horses dragging an ar-tillery piece that collided momentarily with a baggage wagon. It overturned. The six-horse hitch galloped away.

The big black man, mounted on a saddled horse and leading a second mount, surprised Gideon by emerging from the trees. Sliding off with only a guttural sound, the man effortlessly lifted Gideon like a baby. He slipped a foot into the stirrup and eased into the saddle.

Gideon felt something sticky. A brief glance showed him

that a bleeding Yankee soldier had recently fallen from the horse. Gideon first thought his benefactor had killed the riders, but common sense quickly told him that the horses had been captured after their masters fell.

Gideon expected the black man to swing up behind him; instead, he turned and motioned for his father to mount the second animal. He did, patting the area behind him to indicate the stranger should ride there.

The man shook his head, gave father and son a quick smile, then slapped both hands down on the rumps of each horse. They leaped ahead so suddenly that Gideon nearly lost his seat.

Then the horses were running hard, their hooves drumming on the earth, passing the empty railroad cars and carriages that had brought the Yankee women to picnic and to watch men die.

Earlier, they had been laughing and shouting, "On to Richmond!" Now they stood uncertainly, watching the fleeing animals, hearing small-arms fire coming closer and seeing soldiers running toward Washington in defeat.

Gideon held on tight, leaning over the neck of his straining horse, feeling the sting of mane against his face. Side by side, he and his father raced away from Centreville, their horses' noses pointed toward safety in the Shenandoah, Daughter of the Stars.

MORE HARD
CHOICES

After riding all night and through most of the day, bone-weary Gideon was almost asleep in the saddle when his father's sudden whisper jarred him wide awake.

"Gideon, rein up!"

Instantly, he obeyed, shaking off his tiredness and ignoring his still-aching head. He saw his father standing in the stirrups of the borrowed Union cavalry mount, staring at something in the distance.

The boy's eyes vainly probed that direction. He had lost track of the time it had taken to ride horseback through the beautiful valley of the Shenandoah before turning east toward Church Creek. A short but hard rain had soaked his father and him, including his bandage. He had thrown that away, but mud still covered the riders and their mounts.

"Papa, what is it. . . ?" he began, then interrupted himself. He took another hard look. "That's our place!"

He started to let out a joyous yell, but his father's hard hand clamped down hard on his arm. "Quiet!"

Startled, Gideon looked again and sucked in his breath. Several horsemen in blue uniforms rode slowly away, their backs to the Tugwells.

"Yankees!" The word escaped Gideon's lips. His gaze shifted slightly toward the Tugwell farm, hidden among the trees in the river bottom. "Papa!" he whispered, although the troopers were too far away to hear. "Do you think they found our house?"

"I sure hope not." Mr. Tugwell pulled on his horse's right rein. "Let's get off this road and into the trees before one of them looks back and sees us."

Only when the Tugwells were within the sheltering woods did Gideon realize he had been holding his breath. His heart throbbed so fast that his headache felt worse, but he ignored such minor pains. He strained to see ahead, eyes probing the deepening shadows, seeking a glimpse of his mother or siblings.

Mr. Tugwell kicked against his horse's flanks to force the weary animal into a gallop. Gideon did the same, dodging among the trees and leaning over his mount's neck in a vain effort to hurry the nearly exhausted animal.

The sudden bawling of the family hounds interrupted. Rock and Red raced into view, furiously charging the strange horses.

"Quiet!" Gideon called softly. "It's all right," he assured them, then sighed with relief. If the dogs were safe, the family probably was, too. The hounds slowed uncertainly.

Ben darted into sight with an ancient muzzle loader longer than he was tall. He started to aim the heavy weapon at the mud-splattered riders.

"Hold it, Ben!" his father called. "It's us!"

The ten-year-old stopped dead still, stared through the lengthening shadows, then dropped the gun. "Papa! Gideon!" he shrieked before turning to call over his shoulder, "Mama! Kate! Lilly! It's them! It's them!"

Gideon didn't mean to lose control, but his eyes fogged with tears as he stiffly slid from the saddle to be engulfed in loving arms.

★ ★ ★ ★ ★

Nat had thought of a way to outwit the slave catcher's vicious hounds. At sunset, William had ridden off on his favorite horse with half a dozen male friends, all similarly mounted. They had enjoyed an impromptu party. The same thing had happened the evening he got tired of waiting for Mr. Tugwell and Gideon to get back. That had spared the scare he had planned against Mrs. Tugwell and the younger children. As night settled over Briarstone, Nat entered the barn with a lantern.

Uncle George stepped out of his living quarters in the adjoining carriage house. "So you're going to do it."

The old man's uncanny sense of knowing what was on Nat's mind distressed him. He had been so careful to tell no one. He didn't want George getting in trouble, so Nat decided to bluff his way.

"I came to saddle another horse." He hung the lantern on a peg and lifted the bridle from where it hung against the wall. He kept his eyes lowered even though he was sure the old man couldn't see them.

The old slave spoke with suspicion in his tone. "I thought young Master William went off earlier this afternoon with some friends?"

"He did, but I'm to take his horse into the village so he can bring still another friend back with him." It was hard for Nat to tell such a bold lie, but he couldn't let George get blamed for contributing to the escape.

The gray-haired man's tone softened. "If you run into some of those pattyrollers while riding such a fine horse, they're going to be mighty suspicious. Unless, of course, you have a pass, properly signed and all."

"I have one." Nat moved as quickly as he dared without seeming to hurry. He spoke softly to the mount while easing the saddle onto the broad back.

Neither Nat nor George said anything more, even when Nat took the reins into his hands and mounted. He nodded to the old man, who bobbed his head in return.

Taking a deep breath and hoping nobody else was watching,

★ ★

Nat guided the horse outside. Instead of following the well-worn path to the big house, Nat turned the other way and disappeared into the night.

* * * * *

In the softly lit Briarstone library, Emily stirred uncomfortably after hearing the item Julie had just read from a newspaper. George had earlier brought it from the village and given it to the mistress's personal maid. When she took it to the woman's room, Aunt Anna had risen from one of her sick spells to join the girls and have the paper read aloud.

There was an unusual brightness to Aunt Anna's eyes as she told her daughter, "Read it again."

"I've already done that twice—"

"Read it!" her mother interrupted in a rare show of authority.

Emily's eyelids closed as though to shut out the images that the reading of the newspaper had created. She opened her eyes and looked around the room at the three personal maids. They stood silently out of the way, ready to serve the mistress and the two girls if needed.

Julie dropped her gaze to the newspaper and leaned closer to the twin coal oil lamps mounted on the wall behind her. She read aloud, " 'Dismay is rampant in Washington over the panic and complete rout of Federal forces by Rebels at Bull Run on Sunday. President Lincoln met with his cabinet, and General McDowell is expected to be relieved of command.' "

"It's over!" Aunt Anna exclaimed. "It's a great victory! The war's over! My husband told me it wouldn't take more than ninety days to whip the Yankees, and he was right."

Emily sat silently, her thoughts filled with fragments of what had been known or rumored about the events at Manassas. There had been minor battles before, but nothing like the massive one near Bull Run Creek.

At first the Confederates had been beaten back. But reinforcements had arrived by rail, and General Thomas Jackson had rallied the troops. Another general, one of the many men who lost his life that day, had yelled, "There stands Jackson like a stone wall! Rally around his Virginians!"

The inexperienced but reinforced Southerners charged back with muskets, bayonets, and fearsome shouts that struck terror into the untried Union soldiers, who fled from such terrifying enemies. Now there was fear in Washington that the victorious Rebels would march right on into the Northern capital twenty-five miles away.

Emily prayed that Brice and her uncle had not been in that fight. But there had been no word from Uncle Silas, and with the mails stopped between North and South, there might not be any news about Brice until the war ended. Or was it already over?

"Go on," Aunt Anna instructed her daughter.

Julie glanced at Emily as if to show she knew what pain the story must be causing Emily before reading again. " 'The United States Senate, following the House action of the day before, has passed a resolution declaring that the present war is being fought to maintain the Union and Constitution, and not to interfere with such old institutions as slavery.' "

Aunt Anna made a most unladylike noise of contempt. "My husband certainly wouldn't believe that, and neither do I." She turned to the maid standing behind her. "Flossie, run out front and make sure that our new Confederate flag is flying! Keep it displayed night and day so that when the master returns, that's one of the first things he sees!"

When the maid ran out, Emily got to her feet. "Aunt Anna, may I please be excused?"

"Of course. You must have a lot to think about, knowing your President Lincoln and all his tyrannical Union supporters have lost the war so quickly."

Emily bit her tongue and started to leave but met Flossie running back down the wide hall, her eyes wide with fright.

★ ★

"Miz Lodge! Miz Lodge!" she cried, dashing up to the mistress. "I done heerd horse sojers a-comin'! I think they's Yankee dogs!"

"Impossible!" her mistress snapped. "Don't lie to me, Flossie!"

"I ain't. . . ."

"Did you make sure that flag is still up?" Mrs. Lodge interrupted.

"No, I got so skeered—"

"Then get back out there and do what I told you!"

Emily was surprised at how a little excitement over a Confederate victory had made her aunt so animated. She had taken command in her husband's and son's absence. Shaking her head in wonder, Emily climbed the broad stairs toward the bedchambers.

Hearing a faint jingle of metal and the squeak of leather, she froze, one foot in the air like a dog on point at a game bird. "Can't be!" she whispered aloud.

Still, she couldn't resist running to the window at the top of the stairs and looking out into the vast darkness. She could see nothing except the dark bulk of the great trees lining the pathway from the public road.

She listened intently, then shook her head. *I guess I'm imagining things.* She went on to her bedroom.

★ ★ ★ ★ ★

Nat figured his chances of encountering the dreaded white patrollers would be minimized if he stayed off the few roads. He turned the horse in a southeast direction, aiming toward the peninsula Gideon had told him about between the James and York Rivers. If Nat could avoid Confederate troops, he would reach General Benjamin Butler's lines to become one of the Union's "contraband."

Nat's horse suddenly whinnied and another answered. Nat yanked hard on the reins to turn around but stopped when a

★ ★

voice called. "Halt! Who goes there?"

Nat was ready for a possible encounter with Yankee cavalrymen. He imitated a frightened slave. "Don' shoot, Massa! I's jis' a poh' black man a-goin' to do what muh massa tol' me to."

A match flared, glowing against the faces of two young mounted troopers in blue uniforms. The light reflected off the naked barrels of their pistols.

"You live around here?" one of the men asked.

"Yessuh." Nat deliberately pointed away from the Tugwells' home and Briarstone.

The Yankees consulted each other in hurried whispers. Before the match went out and another flared, Nat had seen enough to show they were not much older than he. They were obviously muddy, tired, and probably hungry. In their frantic escape from Manassas, they must have been separated from their command and fled the wrong way.

One soldier held the match close for a better look at the black man's face. "We need fresh horses and something to eat. Point us toward the best place to get those things, and we'll let you live."

Again, Nat was ready. He glanced at the North Star and mentally visualized the swamp. He would direct them into it on the side opposite the Tugwells' farm. Nat quickly gave directions that would make the soldiers miss seeing either Briarstone or the Tugwell home.

The two troopers again held a whispered conversation before striking a final match. In its light, the one who had done all the speaking declared, "We think you're lying to us. But we Yankees don't have nothin' against you slaves, so we're going to let you go, after I trade my horse for yours."

Nat needed no prompting, but when he had ridden out of earshot on the jaded Union horse, he stopped and looked back. The cavalrymen were ignoring his directions. Instead, they were heading straight toward Briarstone.

A terrible sense of guilt struck Nat. He tried to shake it off,

★ ★

reminding himself that he was escaping to freedom. So far, nobody had followed him, and he had not seen any pattyrollers. But he knew that only the girls and the mistress were home alone, and the soldiers were heading that way. Of course, they might get lost again, or miss Briarstone. But what if they found it?

Both white girls had been nice to him, especially the blond Yankee girl called Emily. She should be warned, but Nat was the only one who could do that. Returning, no matter why, would certainly result in a severe whipping for being off the plantation without permission.

Nat muttered to himself, "I don't owe those white folks anything. They're not my concern. I owe it to myself and my family to escape. Then I can try to return and rescue my family."

He didn't want to remember how Emily had pleaded on behalf of the slave mother and her children at the auction where he was sold, but the scene replayed in his head. He tried not to think how Gideon's geography lessons had made it possible for escape.

For a moment Nat sat silently in the darkness. Then he urged his horse into motion.

★　★　★　★　★

Gideon's mother fussed over him and her husband, hurriedly whipping up cornbread and slicing some bacon while they related the experiences that had delayed them for days and nearly cost their lives. She had answered their first anxious question by assuring them that William had not been by or tried to burn them out.

Lilly crawled down from her father's lap to push by her sister and brother where they sat on the floor listening intently. Gideon lifted the four-year-old up on his knee and continued his story.

"The last time I looked back, it seemed as if the whole Union army was trying to outdo each other in running back to

★　★

Washington. The soldiers on foot were run off the road by men driving ambulances or anything else that had wheels. You should have seen those fancy ladies from Washington trying to get out of the way. They were screaming and trying to run in those big hoopskirts."

Mr. Tugwell added, "In the Shenandoah, a man who had a friend who's a telegrapher told us that our troops captured a senator and a congressman. They had also come to picnic and see the Yankees try to beat us."

Mrs. Tugwell slid the cornbread into the oven to bake. "You're sure the gold is safe?"

Her husband nodded. "Safer where I buried it in the woods than if I had tried to take it with us. I just hope to get back there in a few days and dig it up again."

Kate asked, "Will it be enough for us next winter? You have to buy another mule to replace Napoleon, and another to replace that mean one Mr. Cobb loaned you."

Her father put his arms around her and drew her close. "It will be hard, but maybe Cobb will take one of those Union horses in trade. They're like 'contraband,' as that Federal general calls escaped slaves. Anyway, I'm just powerful glad that your brother and I are alive and home with you all. We'll get by somehow."

"I wish we knew if Isham's all right," Mrs. Tugwell said, using her apron to wipe her hands.

"So do I," her husband agreed, his voice suddenly soft and low.

"I wonder about that black man who helped us," Gideon said.

"Me too." His father sighed gently. "If it hadn't been for him, we maybe couldn't have saved your life."

Rock and Red suddenly burst out from under the porch, baying loudly as they charged down the lane toward the public road.

Gideon glanced at his father and knew he was thinking

about earlier seeing the Federal cavalry in the distance. Mr. Tugwell reached for the musket that usually was suspended over the front door before he muttered under his breath. It had been lost at Manassas.

"No gun!" he exclaimed, looking at his family. "All of you get down on the floor and—"

"In the house!" a male voice hailed from down the lane. "Call off your dogs!"

Gideon cocked his head. "Papa, that sounds like William's body servant!"

"Who are you?" Mr. Tugwell shouted through the door.

"My name is Nat. I'm from Briarstone!"

"Come on in!" Mr. Tugwell called. "Martha, light the lantern, quick! Gideon, call your dogs back and come with me. The rest of you, stay low until I see what he wants."

When the dogs were quiet, Gideon followed his father toward the approaching horseman. Tugwell held the lantern high so Nat could be seen where he sat on horseback.

"Yankee cavalry are heading for Briarstone!" he blurted. "Young William is away with his friends, the overseer is in the village, so there's not a white man on the place. The mistress and two girls are there alone."

Gideon anxiously glanced at his father, knowing both were thinking the same thing: Should they stay to protect their own place if the Yankees came, or should they try helping a woman and two young girls?

TERROR IN THE NIGHT

Emily sat on the edge of Julie's high bed and watched her choose clothes to wear the next day.

"Mama is certainly excited," Julie observed. "She expects Papa home shortly now that the war's over."

Emily didn't answer. She slid off the bed and walked to the window. A pale slice of moon cast a cold light over the plantation. The coldness matched Emily's own feelings. She couldn't believe it was over that quickly.

Suddenly, she saw shadows flickering in and out of the open spaces between the great trees that lined the long drive from the public road to the manor house. She whispered urgently, "Julie, come here!"

Julie hurriedly joined her at the window. The shadows under the trees turned into horsemen, riding fast toward the house.

"It's William and his friends," his sister announced. "They're the only ones who would run horses that fast in poor moonlight."

Emily started to nod, then froze. The riders passed between a large, open space between the trees so the moon clearly showed six men. One of them carried a Union flag.

"Yankees!" Julie cried in alarm and dashed out of the room shouting, "Mama! Mama! Yankees are outside!"

Emily followed her cousin into the hallway, where Aunt

★ ★

Anna was hurriedly leaving her room as her maid tried to help her struggle into a dressing gown.

"Are you sure?" Aunt Anna asked anxiously.

"Positive, Mama! Emily and I both saw them riding up the drive from the public road, heading straight here!"

"That's right," Emily declared firmly.

"What'll we do, Mama?"

Aunt Anna's hands trembled as she tied the belt around her gown. "I don't know! Oh, I wish your father were here!"

Soldiers could be heard stopping their horses at the front door. Someone pounded on the large door with what sounded like a musket butt.

"Open up!" a man's voice demanded loudly.

"Mama!" Julie cried. "We've got to do something!"

"I know, but I thought we would have more warning so that we could escape. . . ."

"Open up, I say!" the voice demanded loudly. "Open up, or we'll break it down!"

Emily felt sorry for her aunt, who struggled to make a decision.

"Ignore them!" she cried. "Maybe they'll go away." Her right hand flitted nervously to cover her mouth.

She turned to her personal servant, who stood in the doorway of the bedchamber, the whites of her eyes showing. "Flossie, don't just stand there! Get something to put against this door in case those devils break in!"

Flossie screeched in terror and fled wildly down the long hallway toward the back of the house, ignoring her mistress's orders to come back.

Aunt Anna turned to the girls. "Quickly, come with me!" She motioned frantically for them to enter her bedchamber.

"Last chance!" the voice called. The pounding on the door intensified. "We're going to burn this place down around your heads!"

Julie was about to slam the door while Emily looked around

★ ★

for something heavy that could be shoved up against it. Aunt Anna gasped, clutched at her chest, and collapsed in the rocker near her bed.

"She'll be all right," Julie assured Emily. "It's just one of her spells. But those terrible men. . . !" She jerked her head toward the soldiers. "Do you think they really would burn us out?"

Emily's mind spun wildly in a moment of indecision. Then she took a quick, deep breath. "I'll go down and talk to them."

"No, you mustn't!" Julie cried.

"It'll be all right. I'll tell them where I'm from. They're Union men, so I know they're honorable."

"No, please don't! You know what could happen—"

"We can't chance having them burn this place!" Emily ignored her cousin's further protests and aunt's low moaning sounds. Emily raced down the stairs toward the door, now starting to splinter under heavy blows.

★　★　★　★　★

Gideon's parents agonized over what to do in response to Nat's alarming news about the women being alone at Briarstone.

Mr. Tugwell made a decision. "There's no choice. The soldiers probably won't see our house, but they certainly will see Briarstone. I'll stay here just in case, and you two boys ride to warn those women."

After quickly saddling the Union horse that Gideon had ridden from Manassas, he and Nat rode hard toward Briarstone while Gideon's thoughts raced with them.

He realized that he and Nat needed a plan if the soldiers were already at Briarstone. An idea leaped fully developed into his mind. He rode alongside Nat to explain.

★　★　★　★　★

Emily cautiously opened the door, now badly scarred from

★　★

the blows of the musket stock. She glimpsed the six troopers in their blue uniforms with the yellow piping of Union cavalry-men. One held the red, white, and blue flag Emily knew and had loved all her life. But she sucked in her breath at the sight of another soldier with a pitch pine torch sputtering in the night.

As she stepped out onto the porch between the stately white Corinthian columns, the men fell silent. Emily stopped by the new Confederate flag where it sagged against its staff on the nearest white column.

"She's just a girl," exclaimed the surprised young man who had been pounding on the door with the musket.

"I am twelve," Emily announced with a calmness she did not feel. She boldly looked from one man to the other before focusing on the officer sitting on his horse ahead of the other five mounts.

"My name is Emily Lodge, and I'm from Illinois," she said, keeping her voice steady. "This is my uncle and aunt's home, but no one is here except my invalid aunt and my cousin Julie."

"You expect us to believe that?" the man with the torch swung it closer to cast a better light on her face. "We're going in and searching for weapons and food!"

"Sergeant," the youthful leader with lieutenant's bars on his uniform said tartly, "I'm in charge here."

Emily caught a low but derisive snicker from the older ser-geant. She guessed he resented the officer in his late teens who had probably been elected to rank because of his popularity with the other men.

"We have no weapons," Emily explained, "and I have as-sured my relatives that Federal soldiers are gentlemen and will behave themselves accordingly."

The sergeant muttered, "Lieutenant, you're not going to believe her, are you?"

Annoyed, Emily snapped, "I am a Christian and would not lie to you. It seems to me, Sergeant, that you are talking mighty bravely with five armed men against two girls and a semi-invalid woman!"

The sergeant laughed. "You're a saucy one for a Secessh gal!"

"I am not a secessionist!" Emily declared, her violet eyes burning into the offending speaker.

"No?" the sergeant growled. "Whatever you are, I'll bet you run when I burn this dirty rag." He extended the torch toward the new Confederate flag.

Hot words leaped from the girl's mouth. "I heard how well your friends ran at Manassas, and I suspect you were a part of that, only you ran the wrong way!"

"Lieutenant, let's stop this talking and get on with it!" the sergeant roared.

The young officer shifted uneasily in the saddle.

Emily moved her gaze to him. "Sir, if you are in charge of these men, please be so kind as to lead them away from here at once. Your presence is causing my aunt great physical distress."

The lieutenant replied, "Your accent convinces me of the truth of your origin. However, my men and I are lost, hungry, tired, and apparently in the heart of Rebel country. Although I would like to honor your request, I'm sure you understand that we must take what we need as a necessity of war."

"Well said, Lieutenant," the sergeant exclaimed. "Now, stand aside, or we'll ride these horses right over you and into your big, fancy house!"

"That's enough, Sergeant!" the officer said firmly, apparently shamed into taking charge. "We'll just walk through and take what—"

He stopped at the sound of rapidly approaching hoofbeats. "Who's that?" he asked Emily.

"I have no idea. . . ." She hesitated as a thought streaked into her mind. "Unless," she said slyly, "it's Confederate cavalry."

★ ★

From the road there came a high, wavering yell that made gooseflesh form on the girl's arms. While the sound still ripped the night's stillness to shreds, it was echoed by another similar cry from off to the right, across the nearest tobacco field.

The fearsome cry erupted again to be echoed from the tobacco field. The rapid sound of hoofbeats made the Union cavalrymen uneasy. They turned their horses toward the lane leading to the public road.

"Wait!" the sergeant exclaimed. "Lieutenant, that's only one, maybe two horses!"

The officer hesitated while Emily held her breath. "I believe you're right, Sergeant."

" 'Course I am!" He again lifted the flame toward the Confederate flag.

"Wait!" The lieutenant's sharp order stopped the sergeant's arm short of the flag. "Listen!"

Emily heard it, too. It sounded like a couple of riders were cutting through the tobacco fields toward the barn. But there were also several other hoofbeats that could be heard drumming on the public road.

"There's a bunch of them coming!" the sergeant exclaimed. "Riding hard, too!"

The wild yells again splintered the night from both sides of the great house, making the back of Emily's neck crawl with fear. But this time the yells were echoed from the other horsemen thundering through the night.

The lieutenant raised his voice. "There are too many of them. Sergeant, lead off before we get trapped!"

A mighty sob of relief shook Emily's body as the six Federals raced back the way they had come. She sagged weakly against the door, not understanding what had happened, but murmuring a prayer of gratitude.

★ ★ ★ ★ ★

★ ★

Gideon's compassion swelled in his throat upon trotting the borrowed Federal horse around the big house to where Emily leaned against the pillar. He leaped off the winded horse now white with foam from the hard run.

"Emily!" he exclaimed, running up to her. "Are you all right?"

"Oh, Gideon!" she whispered, turning to him with tears in her eyes. "I was so frightened!"

Gideon didn't know what to do. He dropped his gaze, fearful that she would see the wetness of his own eyes.

He and Nat had charged through Briarwood's tobacco plants, unmindful of the damage being done to the broad leaves growing across between the rows.

Gideon's throat ached from imitating the awesome Confederate yell he had heard when they chased the bluecoats away from Bull Run Creek, Manassas, and Centreville toward Washington. He was sure Nat's throat was also sore from imitating the cry before he turned off to the barn.

Gideon could not understand who the several riders were that had also picked up the yell and charged through the moonlight.

Julie rushed through the front door and threw her arms around Emily, but she blinked in surprise at seeing Gideon. "Where did you come from?"

"Tell you later," he replied, taking another close look at Emily. "If you're sure you're all right," he said gently, "I'd better leave before William comes back."

"Too late for that," Julie announced as several riders dashed from under the trees and reined in their horses before the front door.

"You!" William cried, leaping from his horse with its sides heaving from exertion. "I told you to never speak to her again!"

"Now, just a minute!" Emily's voice returned with a sudden rush of strength. "He just saved this plantation from being burned, and possibly our lives, as well!"

★ ★

Eyes flashing with indignation, she advanced two quick steps toward her overbearing older cousin. "While you and your friends were off having fun, Gideon risked his life to save what you should have been protecting."

William drew back, unaccustomed to such force from a girl, but Emily's blood was like a boiling pot of water ready to blow. She could not stop her furious flow of words.

She turned to Gideon, speaking rapidly. "It took me a minute to figure out that it was you out there yelling like a madman, trying to scare those men off!"

As suddenly as it had begun, Emily's emotion dropped, and the words trailed off. "You did such a brave—" Her voice cracked and she turned away to hide the hot tears that scalded her eyes.

Julie drew her arms tighter around Emily but faced Gideon. "Yes," she said softly, her eyes shining. "You really did!"

Gideon stood awkwardly, not knowing what to do.

William spoke quietly. "So you were the one we heard shouting! My friends and I saw the burning torch and figured out what was happening. We also started yelling, hoping to scare them off. But I had no idea it was you."

"I hoped it wasn't more Union cavalry," Gideon admitted, "but I was too busy to worry about it. Well," he started to turn toward his horse, "I'd better be getting back."

William stopped him. "Please wait! I admit I've never liked you, but I have to say you're not all that I thought you were. When you and your father didn't get back by our deadline, tomorrow I was going to . . . never mind. I'll talk to both of you later."

Gideon said firmly, "I can tell you now: Papa isn't going to sell."

"I'm not surprised." William looked around. "Where's my body servant?"

"He helped save your place," Gideon declared flatly, "along with your mother and these girls. If I were you, I wouldn't ask him how he did it, but take my word for it, I couldn't have done it without him."

William thoughtfully squinted at Gideon, as if trying to read his mind. "Well, I owe both of you for tonight."

"I'm obliged," Gideon said, using one of his father's sincere expressions.

Emily reached out and gently touched his arm. "I can never thank you enough."

"Nor I," Julie added softly.

Gideon smiled and swung back into the saddle.

"Say!" William exclaimed, "I just realized that's a Union mount. Where did you get him?"

"It's a long story." Gideon nodded to the girls, then rode off, smiling to himself. He had plenty to think about. In fact, there was enough that he could finally get around to beginning to keep a journal. A writer needed to have one to look back on in years to come.

★ ★

EPILOGUE

From Gideon Tugwell's journal, October 11, 1933

Memories! They flooded back as I finished setting down these lines based on my journal entry so long ago.

Several important historical facts came from what we in the South called the Battle of First Manassas but the Union called Bull Run.

General Thomas Jackson got his nickname of "Stonewall."

The Rebel Yell first heard there is still famous today, although most folks seem to have forgotten how it originated.

There are people who claim that if the Confederates had continued their victory at Manassas and marched right on into Washington, D.C., the South would have won the war. Sometimes I wonder what our country would be like today if that had happened.

But the triumphant Confederates did not pursue the invaders, and the war dragged on another four years.

Personally, I learned one of the great lessons of my young life from the encounter with the Union cavalrymen and Emily that night after the big battle: It's not race, color, or background that determines a person's value, but what that person is like inside. It is written, "As a person thinks, so is he."

The next pages of my wartime journal take me back to what happened next, when I went *Where Bugles Call.*

★ ★

ACKNOWLEDGMENTS

The author wishes to thank the following people for help in gathering factual information for this series:

Wayne and Theresa Sawyer, for suggestions and materials on historic Virginia sites; Spike Knuth, Commonwealth of Virginia, Department of Game and Inland Fisheries, for pertinent data on Virginia's fishes, birds, reptiles, and animals; Frances Pollard, head librarian, Virginia Historical Society, for guidance in locating all kinds of significant documents; Stephen Leach, a teenager of The Plains, for helpful research; Tony Bernicchi, for resource suggestions; interpretive staff members James Phelps and John Schanzebach at the Manassas National Battlefield Park; and Ruth Kilpatrick, for recollections of tobacco-growing before mechanization.

The author also gratefully acknowledges the importance of these organizations in providing resource data: The Museum of the Confederacy, the Valentine Museum, Richmond Visitors Center, the State Capitol at Richmond, and the Manassas Visitors Center.

Early Teen Fiction Series From
Bethany House Publishers
(Ages 11–14)

———— ∞∞ ————

BETWEEN TWO FLAGS • by Lee Roddy
Join Gideon, Emily, and Nat as they face the struggles
of growing up during the Civil War.

THE ALLISON CHRONICLES • by Melody Carlson
Follow along as Allison O'Brian, the daughter of a
famous 1940s movie star, searches for the truth about
her past and the love of a family.

HIGH HURDLES • by Lauraine Snelling
Show jumper DJ Randall strives to defy the odds and
achieve her dream of winning Olympic Gold.

SUMMERHILL SECRETS • by Beverly Lewis
Fun-loving Merry Hanson encounters mystery and
excitement in Pennsylvania's Amish country.

THE TIME NAVIGATORS • by Gilbert Morris
Travel back in time with Danny and Dixie as they
explore unforgettable moments in history.